Reggie's Plan B

- a dog story -

Reggie's Plan B

– a dog story –

by

Peter Randolph Keim

KeimRanchBooks

Additional Christian Stories
by
Peter Randolph Keim

Available in paperback and ebook
at Amazon.com

Eli's Rock
Charley's Ride
Reggie's Plan B
Mitch's Dream
Bill's Moment
Annie's Wand
Dottie's Boys
Herb's Boat

This is a work of fiction. Names, characters, characters depicted on the cover artwork, places and incidents, are products of the author's imagination or are used fictitiously and are not to be construed as real. Any resemblance to actual events, locales, organizations, or persons living or dead, is entirely coincidental.

Copyright 2012, Mount Vernon WA

All rights reserved.
No part of this book may be reproduced in any form or by any electronic or mechanical means including information storage and retrieval systems, without permission in writing from the author.

First Printing: 2012

Cover Graphics: P. Randolph Keim
Editor: Gini Holcomb

Printed in the United States of America.

For Buff, Lady, Fang, Sam and Luke.
Tippy, Cassy, Sam and Mitsy.
Hank, Hal, Sadie, Gus and Lily.
Riley, Loosie and Rory.

"If there is no Heaven for dogs,
Then I want to go where they go when I die."
- Anonymous -

One

Reggie Barrow wasn't always homeless.

He had a mother and father, obviously. And they had a house, just not a *home*. He had two, much older sisters. They seemed like sisters, were always around. Somewhere around, basement usually.

Reggie's parents had been happy on a couple of occasions, just not *real* happy. It was real funny the day Reggie's father puked spaghetti all over the kitchen, noodles dangling from the kitchen cabinets.

His mother laughed, she was happy His father, not so much, cursed mostly.

Their house was always cold, not the temperature, the cultural atmosphere. They just existed there, day in, day out, time just passed them by.

It was just a house, green paint, some white trim with rusted nails dripping orange and some green mold, broken brick steps. The basement had boarded up windows at ground level. There was glass, but Reggie's father boarded them up from the inside because Reggie's sisters played down there most of the time. Them and their older friends.

Some were cops, some were bikers. They were much older friends. Everybody was older than Reggie. His mother said he was an accident, messed up all their plans. By the time Reggie was seven, he stopped going to school. His mother never checked, his father didn't care. The school made a big fuss from time to time, but eventually gave up.

That's when the cops had a legitimate reason to come to the house. They argued with Reggie's folks night after night, but that usually led to beer and music. One night they had a celebration. Reggie figured they had come to some sort of an agreement, and he no longer had to go to school. But those cops kept coming by like there was unfinished business. It was new cops all the time.

Reggie was swept under the bus.

So, he left.

That was the first time Reggie ran away, he was twelve. His father said good riddance. His mother told her cop friends. The Norman Police found him. It wasn't hard, he hadn't gone very far. He got the snot beat out of him behind a McDonald's, scrounging for food. That's where they found him, in a heap and bloody.

Like every night, Reggie started his food search at the Denny's dumpster. Then, behind Safeway and then Wal-Mart. Hungry, he begged from the folks leaving the McDonald's drive-thru. A big man with hairy arms in a noisy diesel truck grabbed Reggie's shirt collar from the driver's side window. Jerked him hard, headfirst, into the side of the truck's door. Then, hit him over and over with his sledge-hammer fist. So many times his nose broke, split his ear.

Felt like a sledge hammer.

The big guy's girlfriend laughed and threw her half-eaten burger at Reggie. He took it and ran, ate it. He finished gulping it down the same time the Norman Police arrived. They knew him from the house, same cops who spent time with his sisters. They took him to the house. His mother was stoned., her face all messed up. Reggie's dad shrugged, slapped Reggie, yelled something vile, and puked down his front.

From that night on, Reggie only panhandled food from women, small ones. The ones all alone in their cars.

After so many times returning him home from one place or another, the Norman Police took him to a so-so lady with lots of manila files and a brief case and gray hair. She had on two pairs of glasses, one dangling on a rope around her neck. The second pair sat on the end of her nose. She always bent forward peering over the top of the glasses frame. She had big boobs, so Reggie did what he could to get her leaning forward. The lady spent a lot of time on her cell phone. Not about Reggie. Reggie was sure it was a boyfriend. She said only a couple words to Reggie.

After all the paperwork, cops took him back to the house. They just waltzed in like they owned the place, shoved Reggie aside, laughed at Reggie's father and at Reggie's mother, both sprawled out naked on the living room floor.

Puddle of vomit between them.

The next morning, more of the same. Reggie found his father, still naked, hammered out of his mind and more puke, something greenish. His mother? Meth was kicking the hell out of her mind in the basement. Reggie's father woke long enough to clock poor Reggie once across the top of the head, once across the bridge of his nose just as the cops arrived. Reggie's father grabbed a pillow to cover himself, offered the cops a beer.

They took it, always did. They drank beer at all hours, even for breakfast.

There were cops around all day, every day. Some came and went like they were rotating. One would spend an hour in the basement with Reggie's mom or one of his sisters. The other would drink beer, and then he spent some time in the basement. Probably lecturing Reggie's mother and sisters about the evils of meth.

Probably, maybe.

Reggie went to his room at the back of the garage. His nose swollen shut, a purple, black eye, his split ear bleeding again. He sat, rubbed the top of his head, never gave a fleeting thought to his miserable life. Too young for such thoughts.

That's when he found the dog huddled up against the closed, broken garage door. He walked right over the Reggie, crawled right under his one and only blanket, a torn, oil-stained, fuzzy thing Reggie took from the back of a pickup in the Safeway parking lot.

Took a pair of gloves the same way.

Dog had skewered through a hole in the garage wall. There were plenty. Reggie named the dog, Bug. After his favorite car, the VW Bug. Bug was small, not too small, just not big.

Bug cuddled. He was warm. Reggie was cold. Together they were both warm.

The first time Reggie told Bug there was no food, Bug left him. Raced out through the dry rotted hole along the back of the garage wall and came back soon enough. Had half a loaf of bread in his mouth.

Reggie got them water.

Reggie ran away so many times after that, there was always one or more cops bringing him and his dog back to the house. Usually there were cops already there in the basement with his mother explaining stuff. Or in the shower with one of his sisters explaining stuff about something, it always made them grunt and yell. It sounded pretty exciting from time to time. His sisters moved permanently to the basement. Probably needed more lecturing.

The final time Reggie ran away, he was gone two nights. The cops didn't bother looking for him. He came home the third day, afternoon. Bug trotted at his side. From the street corner before the house, Reggie stopped. Bug sat.

No cops. No mother or father.

Sisters gone, too.

No cops in the basement. No basement.

Reggie's miserable house had burned to the ground. To the basement floor. It still smoldered some. Wisps of smoke still drifted into the air, it stunk real bad.

Reggie was conflicted at this development. Sad he no longer had his mat in the garage. Happy he was finally rid of the people he kept running from.

Happy may be too strong, but he felt good, relieved.

He wondered if they all burned in the fire. If so, that would have been good, then he didn't have to kill them. *Kill them?* Something he discussed with Bug from time to time. Chat always ended when they couldn't agree how best to get rid of the bodies.

Reggie sat near the ashes where the garage had been, Bug at his side. He sat a long time, Bug, too. Cops drove by often, Reggie waved, no one stopped, just slowed. Seemed to Reggie, when they saw him they sped away. One did wave, then drove off.

No garage. Only *home* he'd known. Bug's home, too.

The next day, Bug ran off, but came back way too quick with a slab of grilled meat, seared steak, still hot and juicy. Bug dropped it at Reggie's feet and barked his enthusiasm, then ran off. Came back with half a baked potato.

And a really big man Reggie had seen around the neighborhood. Seen him mowing his lawn, pruning his trees, playing with his kids on the mowed lawn and laughing.

"That your dog, Son?"

Reggie had to think about that.

"Yes, I guess he is."

"Dog have a name?"

The man towered over Reggie. A black man, wide as a bus. Baggy pants, white shirt, tight around the collar. Everything was a little tight all around. Shoes were scuffed, looked worn.

"Bug."

"Well, Son, your dog, Bug, took my steak. Then my daughter's potato," the man said. He wasn't angry. He had a soft smile and a twinkle in his eye while he spoke. "Do you figure Bug needs something to drink with that meal?"

Reggie wasn't sure, but the man was smiling bigger now. "You sure it's your steak, Mister? Don't they all look alike?"

The man chuckled and sat on the curb in front of Reggie's ashes that were once his house. He wore a funny collar, Reggie pointed at it.

"You a boss in a church?"

The big man *was* smiling. "Well, of a sort, I guess I am. Not the head honcho, mind you, but people listen to what I have to say."

"You think they hear you?"

"Hear me?" The man thought on that. It was a heck of a question coming from a kid. "I don't know for sure, but I like to think they do. What's your name?"

"Reggie. What's yours?"

"Bob, Pastor Bob. You live here?"

"Here?" Reggie said, looking at the rubble and ash surrounding him. "I did."

"You've been gone a few days, huh, Reggie?"

Reggie nodded.

"You missed the explosion and the fire. May have been for the best. No one died, but it was a big fire. Explosion shook my house around the corner. Luckily, the Norman Police were already in the neighborhood, lots of them. One carried your mother from the basement. Your father disappeared."

"And my sisters? I think I had two."

"Haven't heard or read anything about two girls. Maybe they were visiting family at the time."

Or showering with a cop in the basement, Reggie chuckled to himself.

The big man continued. "You have family nearby here? A place you can go? I don't feel good about leaving you to fend for yourself. Besides, it's the law you be in a, well, a *safe* place. You're too young to be on your own."

"Wichita Falls. Got an aunt there," Reggie lied.

"Could be your sisters are there. You want me to call them for you?"

"Aunt's in jail."

"Oh, sorry. Anyone else?"

Reggie thought for a moment.

"Got an uncle, Uncle Mac. Not far, I can walk."

"You sure? Don't mind driving you, Son."

Nobody ever called Reggie *son*.

"I'm sure. Bug can go there, too."

"Okay, Reggie. But if you need anything, my house is the one with the little white fence and all sorts of toys in the front yard. If I'm not there, I'm the . . . *boss* at the Reformation Church downtown."

Reggie nodded.

Bug did, too.

"Oh, Reggie."

Reggie looked up.

"You be sure to share your steak with Bug."

Reggie's expression didn't change. He nodded he would.

Two

Somehow, through all that jabbering, Bug hadn't devoured the steak or the potato. He just sat, hovering over it like he was guarding it.

Reggie cut the steak into bite-sized pieces and shared them one bite at a time with Bug. He chewed real slow, making it last. They split the potato. That night, they slept between the garage and fence along the house next door. Bug woke them in time to get out before the owner brought out the garbage and discovered them on his property.

Bug was smart that way.

Reggie spent the day sifting through the house's remains, mostly ashes, everything smelled like smoke. He found a belt, some of his sisters' nylons still in their package, liquor bottles in a pile on the torched basement floor. He didn't find any of his stuff, didn't have any.

He did find lots of syringes and condoms.

Reggie sat against the fence smashing bottles into the cement foundation. The shattering glass brought out the neighbor on the other side.

"Kid, get the hell outta there. All kinds of broken glass and drugs and such. The whole mess could blow up again if you ain't careful."

Reggie ran, Bug followed.

They ran and ran.

For sure, not to his aunt's house Wichita Falls, that was over a hundred miles away. Besides, he didn't have an aunt there anyway. One that he knew of. He'd heard talk his mother had a sister in Wichita Falls, but his mother said a lot of things, like carrots came from trees.

Reggie hadn't done much schooling, but he knew carrots came from the ground.

Probably.

He didn't know if he really had an aunt. He knew he didn't have an Uncle Mac. Reggie smiled thinking about his Uncle Mac . . . *McDonald's*.

He had another uncle over near the interstate right where the elevated interstate curved high above the same street where his school was located.

School? How long had it been? He'd forgotten the last time he *visited* West Lindsey Elementary. What? Two years? Four? West Lindsey didn't care for Reggie.

Feeling was mutual.

Uncle Denny had a real nice place of his own. Right there below the interstate. Reggie visited from time to time, but never stayed long. Always crowded. Pancakes and waffles, ends of cold sausage, Reggie's uncle served up lots of those. Best dumpster in town. A boy had to be real small to fit under that chain link fence.

Bug made it look easy.

Reggie returned to his burned-out house and scuffed through the ashes one more time. When he was done, he stepped away to the sidewalk and took one last look where the house once stood, patted Bug on the head. He stuffed his hands into his pockets and started the walk to Uncle Denny's house. Only got to the corner.

"Hey, Reggie."

Reggie stopped. Pastor Bob jogged across the street towards him and Bug. Bug's tail wagged, it never did that for anyone.

"Where you headed?"

"My uncle's house."

"Oh, good for you, Son. Glad to hear that. A boy your age shouldn't be wandering the streets. Hey! You should be in school. You go to West Lindsey?"

A nod that he did. A lie.

"My boys go there, too. Your uncle live near the school?"

He nodded, *yes*. Another lie.

"Good. Well, listen, I hope this all works out for you, Son. It's nice your uncle took you in. Any word about your parents?"

"No."

"I'm sure your uncle will be notified. He's probably at the hospital checking in on your mother right now."

"Yes, I'm sure he is. I'm on my way there right now," Reggie lied.

"Can I drive you? I'm on my way to the church. The hospital's not out of my way at all."

"No."

"You sure? No trouble."

"No."

"Okay, I understand, a little time to yourself, sorting things out. You take care, Reggie. You, too, Bug."

Little dog licked the man's hand. He never did that to anyone.

Reggie panhandled the corner of East Boyd and Classen. Most folks loved his dog. Bug got lots of pats and smiles, Reggie not so much. Very little money made it into his grubby little hands until a woman gave him a long lecture about good nutrition, and a five-dollar bill.

Reggie bought a small bag of cheap dog food and a banana for himself. He loved bananas, especially with peanut butter on them, but he didn't have any. Turns out Bug liked bananas, too.

He should have bought a bunch of bananas.

The next day he worked East Boyd and Classen again until the cops came. Panhandling wasn't illegal, but skipping school was. He knew the cops, they had lots of questions about the fire,

Reggie's mother and sisters. Cared less about Reggie or his father. After too many questions, they took him to Child Protection Services. Pushed him out of the cruiser, one walked him inside, then they sped off.

An angry man in smelly scrubs took Reggie's arm at the armpit and dragged him into a small, glassed room. After more paperwork and a litany of phone calls, a crazy woman with wild red hair, a big tote bag and crooked glasses, arrived to take Reggie to a house where he found himself one of several other kids. Most were older, bigger, all were angry and mean. When the older woman who ran the house wasn't around, they had fun kicking Reggie's ass around one room and then another.

When the redhead with the tote bag came by the next day, one of the big kids said Reggie fell down the stairs during the night. Reggie said it was true. The redhead scolded Reggie to be more careful, her crooked glasses had some tape in the middle above her nose.

The boys beat Reggie again the next night., took him out back and stomped on him, burned his arms with cigarettes and might have killed him.

Bug changed their minds.

Took a chunk out of one guy's hand and another boy's leg, blood everywhere. Reggie and Bug ran. Ran and ran. Reggie laughed. They ate real good at Uncle Denny's house, then Bug tugged on Reggie's hand to follow.

He did.

From uncle's parking lot they walked down West Lindsey. At the corner, high above, the interstate with so many cloverleafs on and off, it made Reggie dizzy. The noise was deafening, cars, trucks, bikers. Reggie followed Bug under the main interstate to the opposite side by the southbound exit to West Lindsey. The exit rose slowly off the interstate, circled high over a manufacturing business parking lot, then it curled back down, made a sweeping turn and exited cars right near Uncle Denny's.

Bug followed a crooked path through tall, uncut grass, to beneath where the interstate exit began its gradual rise. Reggie followed close behind. They both ducked, Reggie crawled. An eighteen-wheeler roared over their heads. Reggie flattened and covered his ears.

Bug smiled.

"What are you smiling at?" Reggie asked.

Bug didn't reply. He led Reggie deep into the oily gravel below. Dark and damp. Concrete, asphalt, dripping oil and fast cars were just above his head. It all smelled something terrible, like the kitchen after his father puked spaghetti.

Bug stopped and sat.

"Is it my turn for the blanket?" Reggie said.

Bug growled, low and gentle.

"Thanks, Bug,"

Reggie never said thanks to anyone.

Reggie scrunched up, his back against the cold, crumbling concrete bulkhead. He leaned back into a recess where the concrete was slowly eroding away between two giant slabs that came together. He pulled his knees tight up under his chin, covered his head with the blanket and thought about the house. His mat in the garage.

Remorse? None. Thoughts of his mother and father? Sisters? None.

Wasn't ever sure they *were* his sisters.

Bug jostled his head under the blanket to join with Reggie. In the dim light, he smiled. Reggie could barely see him. Another truck rumbled overhead, Reggie covered his ears, again.

It started to rain.

And then some wind.

Three

Norman, Oklahoma, not a small town, over a hundred thousand. Big enough for a fourteen-year-old to be swept under the rug if no one's paying attention.

No one's fault, it just was that way, especially when the one being swept, *chooses* to be under the rug.

Reggie had a nice hideout. Cold and damp, but safe, until a frantic man who showed up one night.

Reggie had managed to collect several blankets, a couple pallets and some cardboard. Using a broken hammer he found off the interstate, he chipped and picked at the recess in the concrete bulkhead that supported the interstate overpass. He made it deep enough to fit most of his slender body, sitting up. He hung cardboard to protruding rusted nails with nylon bailing cord. In short order, Reggie had put together a modest hovel that sheltered him from both wind and rain. Not the cold so much.

That was Bug's job, same as making sure no one bothered Reggie, like that frantic man who showed up one night.

Reggie and Bug became non-speaking friends with the young, night shift cook at Uncle Denny's house. They never met face-to-face. Never talked or shouted across West Lindsey, just body language and an unspoken understanding.

He was tall with shoulder-length black hair. He would come out the rear door from the kitchen, wave at Reggie and Bug sitting in the open under the overpass. The wave meant he'd left a package by the dumpster. He'd go about his evening chores sweeping and picking up litter around the restaurant sidewalk and parking lot, then go back inside. Reggie and Bug would across West Lindsey for the plastic bag of leftovers by the dumpster gate. It was enough for them until morning when the nice man did it again on his way home after his shift.

There was always plenty until that crazy-ass, frantic man crashed on the interstate.

The wind was howling something fierce, icy rain raced sideways. The kitchen man at Denny's didn't even come out to do his chores. It meant no dinner that night. It hailed big stuff like baseballs. People were skidding all over the road screaming at each other. There were lots of accidents, sirens everywhere. Caught everyone by surprise.

Especially the frantic man who showed up that night.

He came running from one of the crashed cars just before it caught fire. Ran like the accident was his fault, and he didn't want the cops to catch him. He ran from the interstate right past Reggie and Bug's hovel. Then, abruptly, curled back and dove under the rising asphalt into the musty gloom – Reggie's camp.

For some reason, Bug didn't say a word. Sat deep in the dark where no one could see him. Reggie looked for Bug.

"Bug?" He whispered.

Bug pushed further back, pressed against the concrete bulkhead. This was his job.

The frantic man flattened himself tight to the same bulkhead, peering out at the road every minute or so. He started to slide sideways along the bulkhead, then he shouldered into Reggie's cardboard.

He yanked it aside.

"Hey! That's mine!" Reggie yelped.

Frantic man clobbered him real hard across the face. Hit Reggie's nose and broke it. Reggie cried out and the frantic man smacked him again. Hard enough to knock him over.

"Shut the hell up, Kid."

"You got food?"

"No."

"Little shit liar."

Smack. He grabbed Reggie by the neck and tossed him away from the wall.

Oops.

There was Bug, sitting opposite where Reggie was. Just sitting, tall as he could, tail not wagging. No snarling wolf-teeth. No threatening growl or rush for the jugular. He just sat there.

Glaring.

"Nice dogie. Your dog bite?"

Reggie crawled further away.

Frantic turned, squinted where Reggie was crawling. "*Kid!* I asked you a question. This dog bite?" When he turned back, his nose bumped square into Bug's, cold and wet.

Bug's breath smelled something awful. His eyes weren't all that friendly, either.

Frantic man raised his hand. Bug growled.

Then, too quick to see it coming, Bug snapped with the click of teeth closing. It was surgical.

Took off frantic man's nose. Bug remained seated, swallowed the nose.

The man was screaming all sorts of stuff. Nothing new for Reggie's young ears, but it had been a while since he'd heard such language. He bellowed about pain, about getting the cops on Reggie. Then, he rolled out from under the exit ramp, and ran. Minutes later, three cops on foot were chasing after him in the opposite direction.

"I guess it's time for us to move, Bug."

Dog whined a soft sound, gripped Reggie's hand in his mouth to follow and padded softly out from under the exit ramp. Reggie gathered his blankets and followed.

Not far, actually it was closer to Denny's. Same sort of hideout underneath the road, but this time under the interstate entrance off West Lindsey. Denny's still just across the street.

Reggie thought about his chiseled recess. He liked that. He'd be back.

"We'll have to show our night guy where we are," Reggie said, patting Bug's head. Both were soaked from the rain.

A little later, frantic man was led past them, handcuffed with a big bandage across his face. He led the Norman Police to where he explained a young man ordered his pet wolf to attack him before he could voluntarily turn himself in. Reggie never knew it, but the man was wanted for burglary and rape not three blocks away. He was attempting to escape when he crashed his car.

Maybe Bug knew it.

Four

While Reggie set up their new digs, Bug sat straight and tall for the Uncle Denny's night guy to see their new location. Like a statue, Bug sat as upright as he could until the man spotted him and waved. Then Bug turned back under the overpass to Reggie.

The howling wind made it much colder than it was.

With no cardboard or pallets, Reggie fell asleep shivering, in spite of the warm, red fur of his canine companion. He missed his recess.

When he woke the next morning to honking horns, Reggie was warm on two sides. Bug was curled up against Reggie's stomach as usual. But something really big and toasty was huddled tight to his backside.

It snored.

Into Bug's ear, Reggie whispered. "We're not alone."

Bug turned his head, slopped a big one upside Reggie's nose. Dropped his head back down with an exasperated sigh. Slow and easy, Reggie turned as if on an axis running down his spine. Once on his back, whatever it was next to him didn't stir. It was so big, it blocked his view of the road.

Big-ass something.

And it smelled something awful. Smelled something worse than a wet dog. Its fur was short, gray was best Reggie could tell in the dark. It was big., covered all of Reggie's body length.

Didn't eat me. Kept me and Bug warm. Mostly me.

Reggie had second thoughts, but sat up anyway. So did the new dog. It stretched, snorted some, then turned and sat facing Reggie and Bug. What little light crept in under the road told Reggie the dog was a male and he sat taller than Reggie did. Long ears, big sad face.

Drooled.

"You a friend of Bug's?"

His tail wagged side to side.

"Really?"

Lick.

"Oh, shit!" Reggie wiped the slime from his cheek and forehead, noticed no collar.

Bug sat up to join them. The best Reggie could tell, the two animals had some sort of conversation with all sorts of sounds he didn't know dogs could make. An occasional snuffle, a snort. One growl, but friendly like. Finally, both dogs sat facing Reggie.

"What?"

Neither said anything.

Reggie looked into the eyes of the big newcomer. "If you're stayin', we gotta name you. We'll call you Big. Big and Bug."

Reggie made himself laugh. Bug pawed the ground. Growled a low growl.

"Sorry, Bug and Big."

Lick.

"We're gonna need a lot more food."

Big bolted away and disappeared when he turned into the rain. Bug walked to the edge of the overhead road and sat just out of the rain. He watched for the night guy as the evening grew darker.

Reggie sat, cold as usual. His blankets were great, but when the body is cold and not giving off heat, nothing warms the blankets to reflect back, and so on. He wasn't worried. Never had thoughts that this was all life had to offer him until he died. Just went with . . . whatever. Like, live under the interstate for sixty years. Never thought that.

Big returned, Bug joined him. Helped him drag a big bag of dog food. It was empty of dog food, but filled with pizza scraps, garlic bread sticks, apples and more lettuce and tomatoes than Reggie had ever seen.

"*Pepperoni!*" Reggie applauded. "I love pepperoni."

It's always the simplest of things.

Big glanced over at Bug.

Bug smiled.

Reggie missed didn't see them.

He used his small pocket knife to cut up the apples. Four of them. They shared. Then, Reggie picked out the tomatoes and ate those. "I need salad dressing for lettuce."

The dogs did that glance thing again.

The trio had plenty of water. Reggie had set out three, cut down plastic milk jugs behind the scruffy interstate bushes where no one could see them. Rain collected so Bug and Big could help themselves whenever they wanted. Reggie did the same, but scooped his with a salvaged Starbucks coffee mug.

That first night together was as cold as Reggie had been.

Should be warmer.

Even the tail end of winter could be a real pisser. But early spring weather could be real dangerous on the Plains.

Five

"Hey, Kid! This dog yours?" Said a voice.

Reggie didn't move. Hoped whoever it was couldn't see him huddled low in the dark.

"I *can* see you."

Reggie lifted his head over a crate he used for a table.

"Reggie?"

"P-Pastor Bob?"

"Yep. C'mon out, Son," the big man said. "You'll freeze to death under there."

"I haven't yet," mumbled Reggie, shuffling along on his knees towards Bob.

He stood, shaded his eyes from the low, winter sun. Bob's looming silhouette stood before him. The glare at his back was just peeking out from under angry rain clouds above.

"You living here?"

Nod that he was.

"What happened to the aunt? That Uncle Mac? You can't stay here!"

"Best I can do for now," Reggie said.

"What happened to CPS? They said you left."

"Gave up."

"They don't give up, Reggie. This just isn't right," Bob said, mulling possibilities for Reggie in his mind.

"This big dog. Yours?"

"Yes, Sir. That's Big."

"Big, huh. You had another dog last time we met. Bug or something."

"Yeah, Bug."

"Big and Bug get enough to eat these days?"

"We do alright."

Bob sat, leaned against the bulkhead, tipped his dress hat back of his head.

"Really now, what actually happened with Child Protection Services? I figured you to be under a dry roof, getting three squares a day and back in school."

"Didn't work out."

"Why not?"

"To be honest, I couldn't throw a punch. There was too many of 'em."

"So you just ran? I told you to come get me, didn't I?"

"Yes, Sir. But . . ."

Bob waited for Reggie to finish, he was a patient man, a good listener. Big wandered further out from under the ramp. Looked over at Reggie, slopped a big one on Pastor Bob's cheek.

"Oh, no," Bob said.

He wiped his face with a nasty hanky from his pocket. "He's a big brute, for sure?"

Reggie nodded Big was indeed, a brute.

Bob glared at the skinny boy. "So? Why didn't you come get me? Drop by my church? I know you know where it is, Reggie."

Reggie's eyes dropped to the ground. As much as the hardened, streetwise kid Reggie Barrow thought he was, he was still a fourteen-year-old boy. Small, white and lost.

"Is it trust, Son? Trusting someone? Anyone? Especially the big ones. The adults like your mother and father?"

Reggie nodded, *yes*.

"You hear from them?"

"Yes. They're fine," he lied and Pastor Bob knew it. He knew lots.

"Reggie, your mother died in her sleep. Meth overdose and first degree burns all over her body. Your father's in a Dallas jail cell."

"Oh."

"Look, I can't force you to CPS. I can't make you do anything you don't want to do. You have to make up your own mind, though you're kind of young for anyone to expect you to do that. But as an adult, I have some obligation to see to it you're safe. CPS ain't all bad. Living on the street could end bad. Besides, all the riffraff we have living on the streets, I'm surprised you're still making out all by yourself.

"Then there's all these crazy college kids we have in Norman. We got us over twenty thousand sex-starved, boozin' college kids floating the streets, some up to no good. Most you can trust and mean well, but beer and college kids and a fourteen-year-old just isn't a good mix. And then there's that other element out here on the streets different from college kids, just looking to let off steam. Reggie, there's folks, men mostly, on the streets prowling for stuff I'd rather not mention, but you use your imagination."

Reggie looked over at his two dogs.

"Am I scarin' you, Reggie Barrow?"

"Some, Sir. I think I've been around some of that *element* you mentioned. But I need time to think about CPS. And my dogs here. I leave, what's to . . ."

Before Reggie could finish, a shape emerged to his right. It moved into the sun behind Pastor Bob, casting a long morning shadow straight at Reggie.

Reggie shaded his eyes.

Bob saw the shadow and turned.

Two haunting, baby blue eyes peered from within the dark silhouette along with a mewling whine. The border collie walked slow with a slight limp on the front foreleg. Came right up to Reggie, glanced at Big and Bug, then sat. Put up a paw to Reggie.

He took it.

Pastor Bob saw it all.

"This your dog, too?"

Reggie looked deep into the two, bright azure eyes. They looked back. "Yeah, this is Blue."

"Reggie, dang it, you can't keep every stray that comes your way."

"Yeah, I can. And Blue's not a stray."

"Sure he is."

"She."

"Sorry, *she* is a stray."

"Blue, meet Pastor Bob."

Blue limped the few feet to Bob, put out a paw, Bob took it with raised eyebrows towards Reggie. Then, the Pastor leaned back to the bulkhead, sighed and smiled. "You have a good heart, Son. What are you gonna do?"

"Not sure. Summer's coming, maybe I find work. Maybe with your help, I'll try CPS again. Might even move on down to Wichita Falls."

"Oh, your aunt, right?"

Reggie smiled.

"For your sake, I hope there is an aunt. I'll keep an eye out for you. We'll talk from time to time. You want help with CPS, you know where to find me. No pressure, just want you to know I'm still around. Come by the church. Bring your friends . . ."

"Family."

"Your family. I can get you a fine meal, one for them, too. We serve a meal, free, every Tuesday at five o'clock."

Reggie started to shake his head, *no*.

"And I promise, no CPS, no cops, nothing fancy or tricky. Just lots of folks like you looking for a nice meal. If you trust me, I will not betray you."

Reggie, skepticism slathered all over his face, looked up into the pastor's olive brown eyes. Bob leaned into Reggie's stare, "I will *never* betray you."

Reggie thought. "Can't promise, but we'll think about it," he said.

"Five o'clock if you decide," Pastor Bob stood and walked away after patting each dog's head and a wave to Reggie.

All four watched the big man cross West Lindsey and continue walking away. Big, Bug and Blue sat lined up, staring at Uncle Denny's dumpster. The night shift guy was just leaving work, but stood by his car staring at the dogs.

Reggie stood and waved. The man pointed at the usual drop off spot. Reggie waved at him.

"You guys wait here. I'll get us some breakfast."

Seemed like every time Reggie added another mouth to feed, the night man knew it. There was always enough scraps for the Barrow family. This particular meal, lots of scrambled eggs. A little too much ketchup, but tasty.

Six

The following Tuesday, Reggie spent the day in the woods next to a nearby river. He and the three dogs had made the run across a two-lane frontage road into a freshly plowed field. Stumbled through the rutted furrows to the alder woods behind and sat. The dogs took turns splashing in the shallows. At least one always remained at Reggie's side.

It was peaceful. Where he sat, Reggie watched a flock of birds twist and turn simultaneously, like a school of fish. A farmer was plowing his field further to the north. Reggie frowned at an oil slick in the river. Pop cans and wrappers were strewn about. He thought about picking them all up.

Didn't.

Reggie, reluctant to get into the frigid water, finally sat on a half-submerged boulder and washed his hair. No soap, but it felt good. There was no sun the rest of the day. Clouds roiled across the flat landscape as far as the eye could see. Wind swept the Oklahoma Plains.

"So, do we get us a dinner at Pastor Bob's?" Reggie consulted.

Big swirled his head towards Reggie, a long droop of drool swung as well. It flipped gracefully into the air and slapped the side of Reggie's neck and head.

Big smiled.

Reggie laughed.

Blue licked it off.

"Oh, gross, Blue."

Bug sat, taking it all in.

"So, dinner at the Reformation Church?"

Big nodded he thought it was a good idea.

When they arrived at Pastor Bob's church, there was a long line outside a small, crooked door at the side of the old church. Peeling paint, taped windows and cracked concrete steps didn't seem to bother the folks lined up for food.

Reggie could smell hot something, cooking.

Something hot! How long had it been?

He could hardly stand in line with the dogs, so Reggie and the three canines skirted around the church and came up from around the back where Reggie could watch until the line was gone. But as fast as men and women shuffled inside, more added to the end of the line. Once in a while, Pastor Bob peeked out the door, looked around, then popped back in.

Reggie turned to his pals, then noticed Blue was missing.

"Blue? Come here, Girl."

She appeared from behind the church, Pastor Bob was with her. "Reggie," laughed the big man. "So glad you and . . . your family, could make it. Why don't y'all follow me around back. I have a special entrance for you four."

Cool.

They followed in a single-file line, Big, Bug, Reggie and Blue. They lined up behind the mountain of a man and entered into the church kitchen, the aroma nearly knocked Reggie off his feet. Through the kitchen, down a dark corridor, then down a flight of stairs.

I will never betray you, remembered Reggie, as the walls seemed to close in on him.

Bob opened a door to a room filled with boxes and stacked furniture, old church pews, a weathered pulpit, stacks of books and sports equipment. All used, some pretty old and beat up. In a far corner, a table with two chairs.

"You four wait here. I'll bring dinner," Bob said.

Never betray you.

Reluctant to get too comfortable, Reggie paced amongst the goods. There was a feeling of being trapped, no exit, no quick escape.

He hadn't noticed, but Blue had followed the pastor back up the stairs. Bug sat at the bottom of the stairs, Big at the door to the room.

Pastor Bob returned with a tray. Turkey and a salad with dressing. Mashed potatoes and a piece of pie.

And milk. A tall glass of ice cold milk. Reggie took the glass in his hand, smelled the milk. Sipped it and hummed with delight.

"Be right back with something for the dogs."

But Reggie quickly handed out pieces of turkey to each eager pooch.

Bob returned, three huge bowls of dog food mixed with turkey scraps and gravy. A big bowl of water. And more turkey for Reggie.

Pastor Bob sat. The tired wooden chair creaked under him. He sipped his coffee.

"Lots of people upstairs just like you, Son. No home, no food. Nothing but fading hope that they survive another day. Some are praying they don't wake up the next morning and everyone in between. Most much farther along in years than you."

"I didn't see many kids like me."

"No, you didn't. Not here, anyway," Bob said. "Oh, they're out there, hiding just like you. Scared, alone, maybe with others their age, but they're out there.

"They all lose their families, too?"

With a thin smile, the pastor shook his head at the innocence of the question.

"Some, yes, just like you, but some just ran away. Others, well, twists and turns of life just dealt them a rough road. I get that it's tough out there, real tough, but Reggie, some of those fine folks upstairs had families, jobs, cars and homes, good educations. Then something changed. Temptation fills every nook and cranny of our days and nights. Divorce, drugs, alcohol, the economy, all sorts of things to go wrong and make a man want to quit. A woman, too. But you, Reggie, like so many living in the shadows, scraping for food . . . Reggie, you're too young to quit."

"Not so young, I'm fourteen. And I'm not quitting!"

"So you say, but from where I'm sitting, it looks like you've given up. Living under the freeway with three dogs. Taking scraps from your *Uncle Denny*."

Big looked up from his food, uttered a low growl.

"Sorry about that. The lie, I mean," Reggie said.

"Three really good dogs," Bob said, continued eyeing Big with a wide grin.

Big resumed eating.

"What I'm trying to say . . ."

"I get it, Pastor Bob. But all I have to look back on are my first fourteen years, and they weren't so good. I never even had a real bed. I don't need to give you any more details, you can fill in the blanks for yourself, but from where I sit, you're surrounded by people giving up. You can help *them,* I'm okay for now. Summer's coming. I have more family than I ever did. I have a life I understand, and it understands me, and these guys aren't *just* dogs."

"I can see that, Reggie," Pastor Bob said, realizing he had pushed just a little too far. "You need another piece of pie?"

Reggie nodded eh did.

"More milk, too."

After Bob was out of earshot. "You guys get enough?"

Two smiled, Bug just sat.

"We'll get outta here soon 's I get some more dessert. The extra milk is for you three."

Bob returned with more dessert and milk for Reggie. An extra glass of milk for the dogs. Later, the eating hall all but empty, the kitchen crew finishing up, Pastor Bob stood in the side door watching Reggie and his three cohorts wait for an opening to dash across West Lindsey. He so wanted to help them across, knew he shouldn't. The foursome disappeared down the street.

Just before he turned back into the kitchen, a small, blackish puff of a dog ran out from under a parked truck.

Fell into line behind Blue.

A Pied Piper, Bob thought.

Seven

Buck was a furry little critter with the smallest of steps. He followed Blue and the others across West Lindsey right under the interstate. Huddled quietly next to Big. Reggie hadn't noticed him until the next morning.

"So, looks like we have another mouth to feed, Bug," Reggie said. "Little guy, won't eat much."

A black ball of fur, the little dog came to Reggie, growled low, more of a purr like a cat. Reggie named him Buck. Smallest of the four dogs, Buck instantly huddled close to Reggie. He was a talker. Also, with little resistance, became the alpha dog. His low growls and humming gargles seemed to direct each of the others.

He was also a very light sleeper. Barked at everything that moved or breathed, went crazy over an intruding frog. Reggie finally got up, collected the poor croaker, and put it in a shrub closer to the on-ramp.

"Don't play in the street," Reggie scolded the frog with a smile.

Several weeks passed before a fifth canine, a lanky black lab, joined the troupe as if she'd been there all along. Naming a black lab wasn't too difficult.

Same morning, Pastor Bob slid under the interstate with a large bag of fruit and leftover scones. He said nothing, just clawed his way up next to Reggie, each dog gave him a thorough sniffing over. Big slopped him a good one as usual.

"Where'd the lab come from?"

"Name's Black. She got here this morning just before you."

Bob sighed a long one, his eyes still adjusting to the dark. "Reggie, you can't keep every stray. And you sure are on borrowed time under here. Cops are sure to eventually see you and take you to CPS. I know that's not what you want, but my gosh, five dogs?"

"CPS don't want me. Cops don't either," Reggie said. "I've been round and round with all of 'em. Best I can tell, they've given up on me."

"Don't be so sure. They may have their hands full right now, but sooner or later, Reggie, you'll be back on the radar."

"I suppose."

"Then what will you do with the dogs?"

"Don't know. Best family I ever had, Bob."

That saddened Pastor Bob. "Dinner tonight. I'll have the kitchen prepare something special for your . . . family, if you like."

"Best you check with Buck. Little guy runs everything now. And danged if all the others don't listen to him."

Bob looked down over his raised knees. In the faint light, Buck was but a dark ball of fur sitting straight ahead. Dark eyes twinkled, reflected the light.

"So, Buck, dinner at five?"

Little dog cocked his head to one side.

"That a yes?"

Cocked it to the other side and back again. Then, Buck inexplicably went from dog to dog, noses touched on a couple, not a sound was uttered. Big had to lean his head way down for the connection. Finally, after Buck had studied each pooch, he came to Reggie.

Barked once.

Reggie nodded, *yes*.
Buck returned to Pastor Bob's feet and sat, staring.
Bob looked across the dogs at Reggie. "What?"
"We'll be there," Reggie said.

Dinner was spectacular. Reggie and his family sat deep below the kitchen and the hungry homeless in the eating hall. The day had been warm, finally, warm like spring should be.

Dessert was pumpkin pie. Pastor brought whipped cream for Reggie and the dogs. He also brought another lecture for the young boy and his pals. Reggie, as always, listened attentively. He knew the good pastor only meant for the best for Reggie.

Bob didn't want anything bad to happen to the boy.

But it did.

After dinner, Reggie and his family scuttled across the four lanes of West Lindsey. They made quite a sight, Reggie running backwards to make sure they all made it. Buck leading the line, running his little legs as fast as he could under Big's chin, the others close behind.

Approaching their den as always, jumping from bush to bush, hiding behind the shrub line along the rising concrete exit, Buck uttered a low growl. A couple of huffs and a shallow bark.

"What is it, Buck?"

Voices from under the interstate. Low music, voices and laughter from their home. A girl laughed.

Bug and Blue took off in different directions.

Big leaned up against Reggie's leg.

Buck, as usual, took the point, Black stayed behind.

Reggie dropped and crawled towards their pallets and cardboard. Buck at one side, Big the other.

A small fire lit their faces, two boys and a girl.,not much older than Reggie. They were smoking and drinking, the girl was huddled back into Reggie's recess in the bulkhead. Her laugh was nice. Reggie thought she was cute.

One boy, a heavy one with a thin, scraggly mustache, saw Reggie. "Hey! Get the hell outta here. This is our place." He drew down on a funny looking cigarette.

"No, it's not. I built this. It's mine."

With no warning, the other boy, gaunt in the face, threw his beer bottle at Reggie. Caught him hard in the shoulder. Reggie yelped.

"Shit, he's just a kid like us," the girl said.

"Let's kick his ass," Mustache said.

"No," said the girl.

"Sure, let's," yelled Gaunt.

Before Reggie could collect himself, both boys grabbed him, pushed him hard against the bulkhead. Gaunt punched him in the chest, Mustache slammed his head back into the concrete.

The smell of blood quickly permeated the air.

The girl screamed for them to stop, but both Gaunt and Mustache hammered away at Reggie's limp body.

The girl tried to stop them, Mustache slapped her hard across the face. She screamed and flopped away, crying.

Buck licked her across the cheek.

Black howled like a distant wolf on the prowl.

Bug took a piece out of Gaunt's lower back. He fell back, scrambling in the dirt.

Black looked downright evil in the gloomy dark. Moved towards Mustache, who knelt poised with his arm cocked back to hit Reggie again, but decided he'd better not. He studied the undulating dark.

It growled long and low.

There was something about the low, guttural noise that Mustache didn't like. Stupid as the day is long, Mustache hit Reggie one more time, then started to scuttle out from under.

Black caught his pant's leg. Mustache fell forward, his face slammed into the hard dirt. Big put a paw on his neck. Mustache squirmed, swung at Big, hitting him high on his front shoulder.

Big drooled on the kid, Buck nipped his ear lobe. Mustache cried out.

Buck's piercing yelp echoed under the interstate.

The other four dogs backed off, growling, snarling, lips curled.

The two losers scrambled out from under and ran, each held tight to a minor, but painful wound. Neither looked back for the dogs, they just ran.

Big moved up to Reggie's body draped over the edge of a pallet. Blood ran from several cuts, one eye was swollen shut. Buck and Black sidled up to Reggie, both nudged him, prodded his hand to move.

It did.

Then a shallow cry., a whimper from the dark.

The girl.

Blue ran to her side, Bug nudged the back of her head.

"*Stop!*" She screamed, now fighting to sit up. "Stop." She repeated, less vigorous. She watched Reggie move, rub his eye and sit up. "You okay?" She said.

Reggie looked her way, but didn't respond.

"These your dogs?" She asked, now sitting cross-legged, rubbing her red cheek.

Reggie nodded they were.

Buck barked. The other dogs gathered close to Reggie.

"I guess they are," she said. "I'm guessing this is your hangout."

Reggie nodded it was.

"Sorry."

"I guess it was only a matter of time," Reggie mumbled. "I didn't think we could stay here forever, but I guess I never figured this would happen. Cops, yes, other street kids, no. They friends of yours?"

"Sorta. No. Yes. I don't know. Just some guys with pot to hang with," she mumbled. "You from around here? Norman, I mean."

"Yeah."

"Where's your family?"

"Right here."

"You know what I mean, mom and dad."

"Never had any."

She laughed. Her lyrical laugh made Reggie smile, but smiling hurt. He stopped.

"How do you survive? You and your . . . family."

He wanted to smile at the thought of his family. "We get by. What about you?"

"Family's in Frisco. Divorced, then my mother died. My dad's a trucker. He's never home, so I drifted until I hit Norman. Real nice in summer, warm and hot. Winters can be a bitch, though. May head back to the coast. Hey, what's your name?"

"Reggie."

"I'm Sasha."

"Hi."

"Hi."

"You look pretty young to be on the street," she said.

"So do you. I'm older than I look. Be fifteen in September," Reggie said, worried he was sharing too much.

"Me, too, but I'll be fifteen on the fourth of July."

She looked sad.

"What?" Reggie asked.

"Got no place to go, now. You think I could hang here for the night?"

Reggie looked at Buck. The little dog perused the snouts of the others, then turned to Reggie, cocked his head to the right.

"Sure," Reggie said.

"You're kidding, right?" Giggled Sasha.

"Does his face look like he's kidding?" Reggie asked. It hurt, but he smiled.

Sasha squinted into the fading light, but Buck's face was so dark, she couldn't make it out. "He the boss?"

"Totally."

It had been an ugly evening since dinner. Reggie's wounds were mostly superficial, same for Sasha. They all huddled up close together, but Big separated Reggie and Sasha. The other canines lay in the perimeter.

All but Buck. He paced, sat, ears straight up, one swiveling right, then left. Attentive.

"It's alright, Buck," whispered Reggie. "Big's facing her. She moves, we'll know."

It wasn't that, Buck just felt something. Reggie shook his head he didn't know what it was and dropped down on an old, folded beach towel.

"Goodnight, Reggie," Sasha whispered.

He didn't reply.

Buck mewled softly and paced all night.

He felt something.

It came at just before dawn.

There was the usual exhaust from commuters on and off the interstate. Horns, squealing tires, people yelling out their car windows. Hungry crowds in and out of Uncle Denny's, long lines at every visible drive-thru. Coffee, egg sandwiches, rush, rush, rush.

The bottle broke high on the bulkhead, well short of the family, but it spewed fire. The flames splashed across the rough concrete onto the cardboard, the pallets and blankets and Reggie and Sasha.

All five dogs exploded, barking, chasing.

Reggie scrambled to his feet, brushed away the fire on his pant leg. Sasha yelled something, jumped to her feet, pounded her blanket on the fire. Smoke filled their space.

The dogs were chasing.

Reggie ran after them, Big was closing in on one guy, Black was, too. Mustache and Gaunt ran for all they were worth. Mustache fell, Black lay into him. Gaunt made the road, ran straight away, turned as Big gained on him.

Big skidded to a stop.

Gaunt didn't and disappeared under a city bus.

"*Oh, shit!*" Cried Reggie.

Sasha finally crawled out from under the exit ramp. She missed the bus destroying Gaunt. Got to Reggie's side the same time two cars slammed into the back of the bus. In the confusion, Mustache got up and continued running.

At the same time Reggie threw up and the back of the bus blew up.

"My God! What happened?" Sasha asked.

He told her.

"Oh, no."

The first Norman Police car skidded into the scene. More sirens blared in the distance.

"We're screwed," Sasha said, her face at Reggie's shoulder. He turned to her. She was cute. Short blond hair, scruffy, small tattoo below her left ear – a ladybug. Sasha had mall lips that pouted when she said *screwed*.

"Cops?"

"Yeah."

Buck tugged at Reggie's pant leg.

He looked down. "Yeah, I know," Reggie said to him.

"Know what?" Sasha asked.

"We gotta get outta here."

Buck hurried them back. The other four dogs were gathered on the pallets. One pallet and blankets burned black smoke. Reggie collected what he could easily carry, Sasha did the same. As a tight group, the family inched out from under the interstate on the opposite side from the chaos, broken cars and bodies. Traffic was backing up in all directions.

Black smoke billowed from the burning city bus.

More smoke came from under the interstate.

Police, Highway Patrol and Sheriff's Deputies cars circled the scene. Firemen poured water on the flames. A man and his wife in their van waved Reggie's troupe through the stopped cars exiting the interstate. Sasha thanked them. Minutes later, all were safely ensconced deep in the spindly alders by the river.

"That, my friend, was close," Sasha heaved a heavy sigh.

My friend.

Reggie hadn't heard that . . . ever.
"We're friends?" He asked.
"We could be. Shoot, we *should* be."
Buck barked.
"See," Sasha said, smirking.
"Okay. We'll be friends."

Eight

Their night in the alders was wet, cold and downright scary, noises like they'd never heard. The cleanup continued at the interstate exit. Sirens from time to time. Reggie's burned leg woke him once. Sasha lit a match to look at it. "Not too bad, but we should do something about it."

The dogs remained calm all night. Alert, but calm, reassuring for Reggie and Sasha.

Morning smelled like the world had burned., but no more smoke rose from the scene. Sasha remained with the dogs by the river while Reggie made his Uncle Denny's run for breakfast.

It never came.

A new man tossed all the night's leftovers into the dumpster. Never looked in Reggie's direction. Reggie dodged a few cars getting to the rear of Uncle Denny's. The dumpster was locked up. The narrow opening in the chain link was too small for him.

"Damn!"

He checked Safeway across West Lindsey from Uncle Denny's. He'd never been there, but thought it worth a try. He found nothing but vegetables, lettuce, beets, carrots. Lettuce needed dressing. He hated beets. Took the carrots. Found some hard crescent rolls, four boxes of already broken open, fiber cereal. Took those, too.

Cops saw him.

"Hold it, Kid! Come talk to us," said the cop.

Reggie flashed on two thoughts, run.

And run.

He did, into the open loading dock door at the back of Safeway. He pulled up just inside. The cop car peeled out around the corner. Reggie listened as the car's engine whined into the distance. He came back out and jumped from the dock, ran straight into the tall grass behind the store and hunkered down. It wasn't ten minutes when a single cop appeared on the loading dock. Then the patrol car returned. Sat and waited.

Two more showed up at either end of the asphalt road behind the store.

One was a K-9 unit.

A big-ass German Shepherd launched from the back door of the patrol car. Officer held him firm on a leash. The dog immediately began a sweep around the dumpsters, then followed a trail back and forth from the bins to the steps up the dock, back again and towards the open grass field.

Reggie held his breath.

The officer yelled something and unhooked the big-ass dog.

Big-Ass ran straight for Reggie. He ducked. The shepherd hurdled him and kept going. Straight away, curving to the left, then returned to the road behind Safeway. He approached the officer and sat.

The cop shook his head in disappointment, opened the back door to the patrol car and Big-Ass got in. The door closed and the patrol car drove away. The other two cops stood around talking to a man in a filthy apron. They looked over the dumpsters, glared into the field. Finally, they shook hands and drove away.

"What the hell," mumbled Reggie, still slightly shaken at the vision of Big-Ass bearing down on him, then leaping over and away.

Taking no chances, Reggie crept across the field, skirted two baseball fields and slid down to the river. He followed it until it went under the interstate. He came up and slipped behind the decorator bushes, then made his way to West Lindsey. He ran across the intersection to the field and disappeared into the alders.

Dodging left and right as he ran between the tall trees, he was greeted by Bug.

And Pastor Bob.

He'd been visiting with Sasha for quite awhile. "How'd it go?" Pastor asked.

"How'd you find us?" Reggie said, feeling like he was being watched.

"Not hard, Big was sitting at the edge of the woods. After all the fire and fuss, I thought I'd check on you. Your place is all burned out. Then I saw Big, sitting at the base of the alders at the edge of the woods."

Reggie glared at Big. "I suppose he led you right back to here."

"No, actually it was Buck and Blue who brought me right to Sasha."

"Traitors," Reggie scowled.

Always smiling a broad, toothy smile, Pastor Bob was unruffled. "Seeing as you've lost everything, would you and your family like dinner tonight?"

"It's Thursday," Reggie said.

"I know, I'm inviting you and Sasha and all five of your . . ." Bob paused to grin, "*the dogs*, to dinner at my home. My wife is looking forward to meeting you, my kids, too. And we love dogs."

"Why?"

"Why what?" Bob asked.

"Why do you give a damn about me and my dogs? And Sasha?" Reggie sat on a boulder.

"I guess I like you, Reggie. Admire your spunk, your story, your struggle. You're one out of thousands. Did you know that? There are tens of thousands just like you two. You're not alone, Reggie. I'd like to help is all."

"This ain't gonna be all about religion and God and stuff, is it?"

"No," Bob said. "You can do that on your own time."

"I think I'd enjoy a real meal, Reggie. Let's do it," Sasha said.

To Sasha. "You can do whatever you want. We're not married or anything. Just friends."

Sasha frowned.

Bob frowned.

Big and Blue frowned.

"Just friends," Reggie repeated.

"You're so angry today, Reggie," Bob said. "What is it?"

Reggie looked up at the huge man, over at Sasha, then scanned the five curious, furry faces lined up staring at him. He dropped his head and studied his fingers. "I liked that place. It was mine. I mean, I know it wasn't *mine*, but I coulda stayed there awhile." He looked in the direction of the interstate, mumbling. "Almost died in there. Just wish things would stay the same."

Bob nodded that he understood.

Held up a hand to stop Sasha who was about to speak.

Bob spoke, soft, gentle. "Reggie, you're like thousands of kids your age, some younger, some older. Fightin', scratchin' to make it. All of you dealing with a bad break of some kind. But, Reggie, it sure can be better. You just have to want it and prepare yourself to, as we used to say, *go with the flow*. There's no free pass, no one went out of their way to deal you this hand. It just happened, and you're not alone by any stretch. Think of this moment as an opportunity."

"For what?" Reggie interrupted.

"For whatever's next, like dinner at my home. Tonight, five o'clock."

"Pastor Bob," Sasha cut in. "Do you and your wife have something to treat Reggie's burn?" She reached over and yanked up Reggie's pant leg.

"Oh! Not bad, but we can handle it. Sure, bring the burn along. If Reggie's still attached to it, he can come, too." They all paused for a moment for that to sink in. Then Sasha laughed, Bob did, too.

Reggie smiled.

Bug smiled.

Big slopped one on Reggie's wounded ear.

Using as many backstreets as possible, Reggie, Sasha and dogs were a sight to see. A long, single file line, Reggie in the lead, Sasha at the end. In between, a laughable variety of canines.

They arrived a little late after having to track down Blue and Black. A gray cat had unexpectedly appeared on someone's porch. The two had to investigate and the cat made it to the roof of a car in the driveway. It took some coaxing to get Blue and Black to leave it alone. Big could have shaken hands with the cat, but he wasn't interested.

When they arrived at Bob's, his two boys were tossing a baseball back and forth in the front yard. His wife and Bob were sitting on the front steps, each with a cup of coffee. It was cloudy, some sun, but not warm out.

"Hi, you two," Bob said, stepping down to the walkway. "This is my wife, Trisha. Honey, Reggie and Sasha and, well, you guys introduce your family."

Sasha introduced each one. Big held up a paw, Bug did the same.

Black wanted the baseball.

Blue lingered behind the fence hoping to catch a glimpse of the gray cat.

Buck took a dump in the garden.

"Sorry, Bob," Reggie said. "You have some newspaper or something I can use for that?"

"I have some poop bags," Trisha said. "Be right back."

"You two like something warm to drink?"

"Hot chocolate," screamed one of Bob's kids.

Trisha handed Reggie the poop bag and retreated back into the house for hot chocolate.

"How long you figure to stay by the river?" Bob asked.

"Don't know," Reggie said. "I like it alright, but feel pretty exposed. Really like to get back to the first place under the interstate."

"You know, there are shelters in town when things get really bad," Bob said.

"They take dogs?"

"Probably not, but the Humane Society will take 'em."

"Not in my lifetime. If I couldn't get back to get them, those basta . . . those humane guys will kill the dogs."

"Euthanize," Bob said.

"Yeah, that, too." Reggie groused." Don't sound so *humane* to me."

"But they'd be safe," Bob said.

"Until they stopped breathing. No thanks."

The hot chocolate arrived. They sat watching the sun slip out from under the cloud cover, then sink quickly behind the distant horizon.

"Dinner's ready," Trisha announced.

They crowded around a small table meant for six – six people. But add in five dogs between certain seated bodies and everyone's shoulder to shoulder. Buck and Bug sat on ottomans. Big drooled on the table. Black and Blue were content to accept handouts from Bob's two sons.

Lasagna, garlic french bread, salad and brownies for dessert.

The home was warm inside, lots of kids stuff all around. It looked like Bob and his family enjoyed life, games, books, a ping pong table in the basement.

"What's that room, Bob?" Reggie asked about a narrow door off the basement.

"Tiny shelter in case of a tornado. We barely fit, but it's built solid. Just hope we never need it."

Me, too, thought Reggie, realizing he didn't have a small shelter. Not even a wall to hang his hat.

Trisha approached Sasha in the living room. "Would you like a hot shower, Sasha?"

She thought a moment. "A shower? It's been, um, not sure."

"You can. We have a guest bath down the hall all ready for you. C'mon, I'll show you."

Sasha glanced at Reggie. He smiled and nodded. *You don't need my approval,* he thought, but it felt good she thought she did.

Sasha followed Trisha to the bathroom. It was small, a single sink, toilet, a tub with sliding glass doors.

"Here's a towel, washcloth and your own small soap. There's shampoo in the shower. I think you'll enjoy it."

"But Reggie."

"If he is interested, he can take one, too. When you're done," smiled Trisha. Her chocolate brown face beamed with joy for Sasha.

"Okay, but I'd like to leave the door unlocked. Would that be alright?"

"Of course. No one will bother you."

"Thank you."

"You're very welcome. Oh, would you like me to wash your clothes while you bathe?"

Sasha nodded that would be nice.

"You put on the robe behind the door. I'll wait for you to hand me the clothes."

Sasha closed the door, locked it, stripped out of her clothes and handed them through a sliver to Trisha.

When it was his turn, Reggie reluctantly did the same. When their clothes were dry, Sasha said thank you's for them. Reggie waved as he closed the picket fence gate.

"That was good food."

"They are really nice people," Sasha said. "Nice family."

Yeah. Nice home, too. Reggie mulled to himself.

Nine

Over a period of three weeks Reggie, methodically collected used chicken meat boxes from behind an independent grocery store just off West Lindsey. He'd pull the heavy-duty staples, flatten the box and bring them to the hidden camp by the river. With nylon twine he found in a Safeway dumpster, he overlapped the wax-covered boxes and tied them together.

"What are we gonna do with this?" Sasha asked, looking over the six-by-eight sheet of chicken boxes.

"Wax will repel the rain. I figured if we ever get caught in a downpour, the wax won't get soggy like cardboard. We'd stay kinda dry."

"You need more to fit the dogs, too."

"Yeah, need more."

Prophetically wise as he was young, the rains came. Big and long. In fact, the entire weather pattern changed. It was an abrupt change from the expected warmth of spring, back to cold and rain – and unusually strong winds.

It rained for three days and the river rose, but not enough to reach their wax-covered camp. Lightning scared the hell out of them all, even Big. Buck hid for two of the days. Sasha cried and held Reggie's hand. Reggie said nothing about that, just held on. Her hand was warm, soft.

Halfway through the third day, Pastor Bob sloshed his way into the woods and yelled he was arriving so the dogs didn't take him down.

"You kids alright?"

"Yes."

"Yes."

"I could fix you up in the church basement if you'd like. Just until the rain stops."

"You think it ever will?" Sasha asked, kidding a little.

"Weather report isn't good. More thunder and lightning on the way. Looks like if you get much more rain, you'll be under water."

The pastor was yelling over the wind and rain. Sasha squeezed Reggie's hand.

"Why us?" Reggie asked, locking onto Bob's dark eyes.

"Why not?"

"I mean, like you told us, there are kids all over this town living under cardboard. Why us?" Reggie squeezed back.

"Don't read too much into it, Reggie. I've been looking into every dark hovel from my house to here. Sent lots of kids and adults to the church already until this blows over. I just didn't want to leave you out. You guys are still kids in my eyes. There *really* are people of good heart and soul who simply care about others. You're not the only ones I help."

"All those you feed," Reggie said.

"Yes, all them."

"They're all old."

"They were all young like you once."

"I suppose," Reggie agreed.

"Come with me. You can bring the dogs."

"I need to wait here," Reggie insisted.

Pastor Bob, Sasha and probably all the dogs, wanted to ask why. No one did.

"Okay," Bob screamed, thunder rolled across the plains.

Sasha trembled. Bob sat with her as rain ran off his umbrella. He pulled a beaten cell phone from his coat pocket and handed it to Sasha. Small piece of paper was taped to it with a phone number on it. It said, *Bob*. He yelled into her ear. "My cell phone number. That's a prepaid phone. Battery should last quite awhile. Keep it off unless you need it. I have mine in my pocket all the time."

She smiled, mouthed a thank you.

Bob tapped Reggie on the shoulder, then struggled away through the mud and falling tree limbs.

"He's nice," Sasha said.

Reggie didn't respond, but kept his eyes on the big man's shadow disappearing amongst the trees.

"He only wants to help," she said. "Maybe we should take him up on it."

"Maybe. He's still an adult. And . . ." his voice faded into the noise swirling around them.

Reggie turned to face Sasha. "We can't stay here, but I can't move to his church. It's nothing to do with Bob, or it being a church, or God's house, or anything like that. I haven't given any thought to God. If He's real, well, He has it out for me. I'd be a sitting duck at the church. No, I can't go there."

"You go there for food," Sasha reminded.

"I know," he said, feeling a hint of guilt. "The church is Bob's, and Bob is an adult. Right now adults are not on my list of good things."

"He seems . . ."

Reggie squeezed her hand and cut her off. "He *seems* nice. That's just it. My mother *seemed* nice. Even my father was, once or twice. Same for all those horny cops and women who I was told were my sisters. Then they turn on you. Lie, steal and betray. I just can't get by it that there may be a good one out there."

"What about the man who puts out food every night at Uncle Denny's?" Sasha asked. The man had returned, and as usual, left more than enough to feed them all, morning and night.

"Don't know him, never actually met him. I mean, yeah, he does a nice thing, but what's he after?"

"Kinda cynical, don't you think?

"I guess."
"You trust me?" Sasha asked.
"Yes."
"You trust the dogs?"
"With my life."
"Maybe make a little room for Bob."
"Need more than a little. He's really big."
She laughed. "Give it some thought."

Lightning slammed into the field across the river. Thunder shook the ground. Sasha hugged tight to Reggie. The dogs did, too.

We move back tonight, Reggie thought.

And they did.

Reggie and Sasha hauled all they had in one trip. Tied some stuff to Big's back. Someone had removed all the charred pallets and odd debris from under the exit ramp. It had never been cleaner.

Was sure a lot drier.

There was a small leak along the back of Reggie's recess in the bulkhead. He chipped out more and a path for the water to whisk away from where they sat. Sasha slept all night, though the distant thunder and lightning kept her turning side to side. Big cuddled up next to her on one side.

Reggie, for the first time, slept with his back to hers – touching. It felt good, he trusted Sasha.

Bob still had a ways to go.

The next night was Tuesday night dinner at Bob's church. Reggie, Sasha and the dogs ran in the rain to the back door. A man Reggie hadn't met before, let them in.

"Name's Merle. You Reggie?"
"Yes."
"C'mon in, Bob's busy. Asked me to help you guys get to the basement." Merle led the way. He didn't have to.

"I'll get your food," Merle said.
"Thank you," Sasha said.
Bug barked.

Black did, too.

Merle returned, his hands were big, looked swollen, torn up, scarred, but strong. "Here you go, plenty more upstairs. Weather will keep some folks away. We'll have lots to go around. Storm's comin'."

"Isn't *this* a storm?" Sasha asked.

"Not like what they're warning about," Merle replied.

"How bad?" Reggie's antennae went up.

"Bad. Threat of tornadoes. Kinda unusual for these parts this time of year."

"Yeah," Reggie said, silently thanking himself for moving the family back under the road before the storm hit town.

"What do you do, Merle?" Sasha asked.

"I'm a mason."

Both Sasha and Reggie looked blank.

Merle laughed. "A mason. I build stuff with bricks, stone, cement, tile. Like you have in a kitchen or entry by the front door. Fireplaces, outdoor barbecues, stuff like that."

Reggie smiled. He couldn't remember any mason stuff in the house. "You like it?"

"Yes, I do. Just wish there was more work. This building recession has made it pretty hard to find work. Oh, I'm not complaining, I get my share, but in boom times, it's crazy and fun. Kinda like doing artwork with stone."

Merle turned to leave.

"Merle?"

"Yeah."

"I'll be fifteen pretty soon," Reggie said, trying to sound as adult as he could. "I'm a school dropout, but I'm not afraid to work. I'm kinda creative with my hands. Is there something I could do when you work? Haul the bricks, get coffee, whatever."

Merle laughed. "I started out in this business doin' odd stuff like that. My dad was a mason and a damned good one, too. Taught me a lot. Mostly how to stay out of the way and not get smashed by something real heavy. My first real job with him was cutting tiles. It's not rocket science. I started with easy square cuts I could handle. Went from there."

"So, are you saying, yes? I'd work real cheap," Reggie said.

"You sure would," laughed Merle.

"How old were you when you started?"

He laughed even harder. "Right after I dropped out of high school, about fifteen." Merle gathered up the trays, his kitchen towel and left for the kitchen.

Reggie was deep in thought.

"What are you thinking?" Sasha asked.

Reggie sat down on the floor to pet two of the dogs.

"Artwork with stone."

"Maybe something you could learn."

"Yeah, maybe."

He scratched behind Bug's ears.

Thunder shook the old building. Some light, fine dust lifted off some of the stored furniture.

Lightning flashed.

Sasha studied the ceiling as if it was about to drop on them.

Ten

For the next few days, Reggie chipped the recess even deeper. Enough for one of them to push into and be completely out of sight. Didn't know why, just something to do. He found a pallet near a flooring store. Hauled it back for a table, of sorts. They didn't need blankets anymore, the temperature was much warmer. Between the seven of them all cuddled up, they were plenty warm.

The weekend was hot, unusually hot. The dogs lay in the cool shade under the interstate, all were panting. Reggie filled all the cut down jugs with cold, river water. He and Sasha took a walk hoping to scare up some mid-day chow.

Wherever they went, folks were in t-shirts and shorts, flip-flops. Talking about the weather, global warming, crops failing, water rationing.

"Water rationing? River's flowing near the top. There's plenty," Reggie said, as if he knew anything about it.

Sasha had peeled off her hoody sweatshirt, then her long sleeve polo from Salvation Army and finally, down to her striped tank top. She had no bra. She sat in the grass behind Safeway, her back against a pile of rocks somebody must have pulled from the field. Reggie stood next to her. Was about to say something when he noticed her.

Actually noticed her.

He hadn't really seen her in the sun.

Noticed her hair, blond like a surfer, cropped short, her ears showed. Both were pierced with a small pearl. No part, just scrambled. It had a luster about it he liked.

Noticed her flawless face, smooth, kind of creamy cheeks. Probably soft to touch, he hadn't done that yet.

Touched her.

Her neck was long. It, too, looked real soft. She had creases that ran horizontal across her throat, a couple of them. Reggie liked them, but not sure why.

Her hands were folded together against her chest, like in prayer. They were small, delicate, but calloused and weathered from the street life. Reggie nodded slightly, Sasha was real pretty. It made him think.

"We ought to go see that Merle guy, the mason."

Sasha opened her eyes. Shaded them to the brightness. Reggie studied her dark, almost black eyes. Such a contrast to all her blondness.

"You thinking maybe you might get some work?"

"Maybe. At least we could see where he works. He said it was three blocks south on tenth. You wanna go?"

"Sure."

He helped her up. Held her hand a long time.

"What?" She asked.

He shook his head it was noting, but he flushed a little. "Nothin'." He let go, turned away to go. Sasha caught his hand. Adjusted her grip until they were holding firmly.

Reggie didn't look at her.

Nor she, him.

They found Mike and Son Masonry.

"I thought his name was Merle?" Sasha said.

"Me, too."

"Mike was my dad," Merle said from behind his heavy-duty truck parked in the driveway by the building. "He's gone now, but I kept the name. Kind of a tribute to him. He was a great guy."

"Your mom?" Nosy Reggie asked.

"Never had one."

"Hah!" Laughed Reggie, though it was how he felt about his mother. "Sure you had a mother."

"Yes, I'm sure I did," Merle kidded. "She's my bookkeeper, inside. C'mon, you should meet her."

They did. Nancy was her name. Nice lady. In a wheelchair, spinal something or other. Gray hair all rolled up in a bun atop her head. Sticks stuck out from it like knitting needles.

She was sharp as a tack, her eyes sparkled with questions.

"So, you thinking of maybe becoming a mason?"

Reggie nodded *maybe* he shrugged.

"Merle would be a great teacher if you do," she said.

She motioned to Reggie to move closer while Merle was explaining tile to Sasha. "He's good to work for if he hires you. Teach you all the tricks of the trade. Never swears, always has your back. And, if he makes you an offer, remember, I do the books. We can afford eight dollars an hour."

"Eight?"

"Shh. He'll offer six, you take seven. Then, when he's happy with you, assuming you do good work, he'll have room to give you a nice raise. He'll feel real good about that and you can feel like you earned it. Everybody wins."

"Wish we could find something for Sasha."

"Can she cook?" Nancy asked. "If so, Merle can use some volunteer help at the church every night. Especially Tuesdays when they serve the dinner. Free food."

Reggie laughed. "Only been with her living on the street. No kitchen, so to be honest, I don't know if she can cook."

"You two involved?" She winked.

Reggie took a deep breath. "Not that I haven't noticed how cool she is, 'cause she is. Real cool, but . . . "

"Afraid?"

"Yes."

"Can I tell you a secret?"

"Sure."

Reggie leaned lower.

"Pastor Bob's been over and told us all about you and your dogs, some of your past. I certainly understand why you might be afraid to make any kind of commitment. Of course, it sounds like you're committed to the dogs."

"Yes, they are family."

"And Sasha?"

Reggie grinned. "Family, too."

"Just remember, Reggie, we never regret committing to the right one."

"How do we know?"

"When you do," she said.

Sasha and Merle appeared in the office door. "Maybe have to hire Sasha instead of Reggie," Merle said.

"That right?" Nancy grinned. "Why's that?"

"She has a real fine color sense. Design, too."

Nancy glanced at Reggie, worried he might be upset by this turn of events, but he wasn't. He was smiling at Sasha's gifts and possibilities.

He's committed, Nancy thought with a chuckle.

"But, can she cook?" Nancy asked.

"Yes," Sasha answered.

"Just thinking out loud," Merle sidestepped. "Reggie, when can you start?"

"You're offering me a job?"

"Yes. Me and Mother just landed all the tile and masonry work at a small, four-home development on the west side of town. All custom work, each home is different. Being framed right now. We start in a month or so. I'm going to need help from somebody."

Reggie looked at Sasha, back to Merle. "But the dogs."

"Bring 'em," Merle said.

"Okay, then," Reggie smiled. Abruptly hugged Sasha. She hugged back, catching Nancy's warm smile behind Reggie. Then, Reggie whispered to Sasha, "*Can* you cook?"

"Totally."

"Well, if so, Mother says Merle may have a part-time job for you. Doesn't pay, but free food for you and me."

Sasha pushed back from Reggie's arms. "Bob's church?"

"Yep. Merle needs help in the kitchen. Need to be there at four to set up."

"But we get free food anyway," Sasha said, then wished she hadn't.

Merle jumped in. "Yes, you do, but I'm there every night making sauces, baking bread, just getting things ready for Tuesday."

"You work every night for one night's dinner?" Sasha asked.

Merle looked at his Mother, who nodded and winked. A suspicious smile. Merle moved a little closer. "No. Actually, I bake bread and make soup for about seventy-five homeless who really need the help. Bob and I pay for it out of our pockets. We keep it quiet, but there would be dinner for you two every night. Scraps for the dogs."

Sasha looked at Merle. Then slipped over to him for a hug. She hugged Nancy, too.

Reggie took Sasha's hand. Both smiled.

On the way back to the interstate, a half-crazed, long-haired kid with a mangled mustache ran them down in the crosswalk.

Eleven

They weren't much, but unlike other homeless kids tramping around Norman, Buster and Mitch O'Connell, aka, Mustache and Gaunt, had wheels. The wheels were balding, but the blue, '92 Oldsmobile Cutlass Ciera ran good. Yes, it burned oil, but the brothers could steal all the oil and gas they'd ever need.

And the four-door beauty made for nice living quarters in the rain and snow.

They kept it in the parking lot of an empty bookstore under the interstate. Moved it every so often. Cops haggled them from time to time, but with so many homeless on the streets, cops would just hustle them along rather than roust them.

The day Mitch made a face plant into the front of the long, green, Norman City Bus, the brothers had siphoned just enough gas from the Olds to fill half a beer bottle, Buster used an old rag for the fuse. They laughed when it spewed all over that damn skinny kid and all those dogs, and that miserable Sasha.

She would have hung with the O'Connell boys for a couple nights, mooching food and an occasional hit on their pot. Buster had been eyeing her and her nice body since she hooked up with them. Had plans to get into her shorts. Then, she decided to hook up with that kid and his dogs.

Those damn dogs.

When he saw his brother's body lift high in the air and sail fifty feet down the frontage road, Buster ran, scared and crying.

Then he wanted some payback.

He followed Reggie and Sasha in the Olds until they reached Mike and Son Masonry. He was surprised and pleased they had no dogs with them. He parked down the street when they went inside the stone shop.

"So, no damn dogs to protect you today," Buster groused to himself, hunkered low in the Olds. "I could kill your skinny ass, grab Sasha and have her in my bed in ten minutes."

He waited.

Stewing in his grief and anger, Buster decided he didn't want to get into Sasha's pants, he wanted her dead, too. Like his brother, Mitch.

Wish I had a bus.

It wasn't long, and the two kids came out of Mike and Son Masonry. They looked happy. Buster's cheeks and neck flushed red when Reggie took her hand. They turned up the street away from where Buster was parked. Made him even more angry.

With a belch of black smoke, the Olds turned over. Buster pulled from the curb to follow. Two blocks up, they turned towards West Lindsey, stopped at the crosswalk and waited for the signal.

Buster crept closer, watched the signal turn yellow for the cross traffic. He inched ahead and when the signal changed, he tromped on the accelerator.

Reggie and Sasha were almost across the lane when Buster hit them, Sasha first. She slammed onto the hood, broke the windshield, then flipped over the roof.

Buster couldn't help his laughter.

When first struck, Sasha hit into Reggie before sliding up onto the hood, into the windshield. Reggie folded in half, his head hitting Sasha's, then he launched forward twenty feet onto the trunk of a parked car.

Buster kept his foot on the pedal, careened by Reggie. Blood blossomed across Reggie's shirt sleeve. In his rear view mirror,

Buster watched Sasha bounce a couple of times before skidding to a halt in the middle of the road. His heart racing, Buster flipped a finger into the mirror.

"That's for Mitch!"

He powered the old car around the next corner heading for his usual parking place under the interstate.

Sasha's right thigh bone snapped at initial impact. Her head bent right, then swung left, cracking into Reggie's head. She heard laughter just before her shoulder broke the car's windshield.

She heard nothing more after her head smacked the roof.

Reggie's head hit Sasha's, then he was airborne. Conscious and flying. So far and high. Then he hit the parked car. It crumpled under the impact. He was facing the street when the blue car passed him. Inside, he saw Mustache, laughing and giving him the finger.

Then everything went dark.

When Reggie woke, his arm was in an awkward brace. The room was all white and clean, an antiseptic smell. Pastor Bob sat in a chair next to the bed. Merle and his mother were there, too.

"So, welcome back to the land of the living," Bob joked.

Reggie turned his head to Bob, "Sasha?"

"In the room next door," Bob said, not smiling as usual. "Hurt real bad. All sorts of things broken, but she'll live."

"It was Mustache."

"Mustache?" Merle asked.

"Yeah, a kid Sasha hung with for a time, before she moved in with me," Reggie struggled to swallow.

"Give him some water, Merle," Nancy said. He did, slow and easy through a straw.

"Him and his brother. Me and Sasha called them Mustache and Gaunt because we didn't know their names. They tried to burn us out."

"The fire under the exit ramp. Your leg burn?" Asked Bob.

Reggie nodded, *yes*.

"When they ran, Gaunt caught the front of a bus. Mustache got away. Me and Sasha and the dogs . . . *oh, shit, the dogs!*"

"They're at my house, Reggie. The boys are having a great time with them. All but Bug, he seems to sense there's something wrong."

"Yeah, he would. Can I see Sasha?"

"I'll get a nurse," Merle said.

Bob moved closer. "We'll keep the dogs until you're ready to get out of here. Then, my friend, it's time for you to find better quarters for you . . . for you and your family."

Reggie only squinted back at Bob. He just wasn't sure yet about all that much trust. A nurse appeared in the doorway.

"She's sleeping right now, but when she wakes, I'll come get you," she said.

"Okay."

"We're going to leave you to rest, Reggie. Be good to take advantage of this place. Clean sheets, three squares and a nice shower," Merle said. "And when you're ready, we'll get you busy with the tile and sand and cement and so on."

"The tile cutter?" Grinned Reggie.

"Yeah, that, too."

They left.

Sasha.

Reggie swung his legs off the bed, he hurt like hell all over. Took one step and was on the floor. The nurse came in, helped him up and back into bed.

"Your right foot's got two broken bones," she told Reggie. "It will take time to heal. That's why I'll come and get you – with a wheelchair."

Reggie forced a smile. "She still asleep?"

"Reggie, it's been two minutes since I said she was asleep, but if you must, I'll wheel you in so you can sit with her. You have to keep quiet though."

He agreed.

Moments later the nurse rolled Reggie into Sasha's room. He gasped, clutched his mouth. Her leg was in a crazy sling, high in the air. Her head was encased in white wrap. What little he could see of her face, Reggie thought someone had painted it purple. Her right arm was in a cast.

"She don't look good," he said.

"She isn't," the nurse mumbled back. "Collapsed lung and she has four broken ribs, as well. And a mild concussion, but nothing appears to be life-threatening."

"I'll be quiet."

"Yes, you will," the nurse scolded.

Bug paced the perimeter of the three-foot, white picket fence surrounding Bob's front yard. Balls and squeaky toys were flying all over the yard. Big was carrying Bob's youngest on his back. Black and Blue were tugging either end of someone's garden glove. Buck sat on the first step down from the porch. Trisha stroked his soft coat.

Walking up the block, Bob led Merle were pushing his mother in her wheelchair.

"So?" Trisha asked, standing to greet them.

Bob filled her in.

"What are we going to do about them?" Trisha asked.

"Don't know," Bod said. "Reggie's pretty stubborn. He's been through some serious issues he can't get past. All we can do is keep trying."

Trisha dropped her head in thought.

"What is it?" Bob asked.

"Why this one?"

"You mean, why Reggie when there are so many?"

She nodded, folded her arms across her chest expecting an answer. Both Merle and Nancy turned to Bob waiting for his reply.

"I really don't know," Bob said, shaking his head. "There's something compelling, crying out, about this particular kid, Sasha, too. Something that keeps me on the hook to help them."

Bug barked.

Bob looked down at the multicolored little dog. "Yes, there's something compelling about you, too, Bug."

Bug smiled.

"Well, if he can work, he'll have a job," Merle said. "And if she lives and can work, Sasha can help with the food at church."

He started pushing Nancy towards the gate.

"I just wish we could scare up a place for them to live," Bob said, more to himself than anyone in particular. "Something Reggie would agree to. Tough with five dogs,"

"We'll ask around," Nancy said before they were too far up the sidewalk.

Bob and his family waved goodbye.

Bug barked, then returned to pacing the fence.

Twelve

Reggie spent the next two days in the hospital. Most of it in Sasha's room holding her hand, watching television. He'd never had one.

Morning of the third day, Pastor Bob visited with Bug. Reggie made it to a bench just outside the sliding front doors and sat with Bob and Bug for a long time. He was feeling much better, he could walk.

"They said I could leave today," Reggie said.

"So, will you?" Bob asked.

"I suppose. It's been nice, me and Sasha, a roof, shower and all. Sure makes me think."

"Yeah, I get that. Been a while."

"No, Bob, I *never* had a roof. A *real* roof."

"The garage had a roof."

"But it was the *garage*," Reggie insisted. "I mean, as far back as I can remember, I was in the garage."

Bob was a little speechless. "You check out today, there'll be no roof 'cept the interstate ramp."

Reggie crinkled his mouth, nodded he knew that.

"I've been talking to Merle and Nancy. You take a job with them, and I'll fix you and Sasha a place in the church basement to stay. It would be real small, but warm and dry. You'd have to pay rent."

"The dogs?"

Bob patted Bug's head.

"Them, too."

As resistant a Reggie was to such rigid confinement and expected routine, something inside told him this might be the right thing to do. "I'll talk to Sasha, but no promises."

"Sure, no promises."

Reggie checked out the next morning. Bob drove him to see Trisha and the kids, the dogs went crazy.

Trisha fixed scrambled eggs, bacon and toast, a basic breakfast for some, died and gone to heaven to Reggie.

"What now, Reggie?" Trisha asked, wafts of steam curled up from her coffee.

"Back to . . . I don't know for sure," he stumbled in thought. "After all this, I kinda hate to drag Sasha back under the interstate, and I like Bob's offer. Not sure why me, but I'm thinking on it."

"Better to think, *why not me,*" Bob said. "We know about all the kids on the streets. Shoot, not all of them are kids, but change of some kind has to start somewhere. Why not with you? And why not Sasha?"

"And the dogs," Reggie added.

Bug looked up at Bob.

"Yeah, the dogs, too," Bob said.

Trisha put a hand on both men's shoulders. "Reggie, why not stay here today and tonight. The dogs are happy and you need another day to think about things."

Reggie, reluctant to accept the obvious handout, nodded he would.

Bob smiled, took Trisha's hand and squeezed. "All you get here is the couch, though."

Reggie actually laughed out loud.

"Look at those clouds," Trisha said, opening the screen door. "Looks like a storm is on the way."

Bob noticed it and shrugged.
Reggie didn't look.
Bug went down the steps and started his pacing.

After a fried chicken dinner, Reggie and Bob sat together watching the end of a baseball game on television. Sometime during the eighth inning, a bulletin crossed the bottom of the screen warning of possible tornadoes.

"We get these warnings all the time," Bob said. "Time to worry is when the warning siren goes off, but then it's almost too late."

"That when you and the family cram into that shelter in the basement?"

"Yes."

"Ever use it?"

"No, it's mostly storage. Kids' toys."

Reggie thought on that a moment. Then Trisha brought them strawberry shortcake and coffee.

The next day, Reggie and Bug fought through the wind to the hospital. Bug waited outside. Reggie met Sasha in the lobby. She was out for a stroll, but still not ready to check out. The cast on her leg and the crutches made getting around difficult. She looked pale.

"You feel as good as you look?" Reggie asked.

"Funny," Sasha said. "I feel like shit."

He took her hand. "Come sit a minute."

They slowly walked to the cafeteria for something to drink. Sat by a window and an actual-size, bronze sculpture of a bison.

"They were sure big," Reggie mumbled.

"Yep."

"Got us an offer from Bob and Trisha . . ."

"Us?" She interrupted.

"Yeah, us. Right now we are *us*. You and me, and a few animals."

"How are they?"

"Great! All at Bob's still, but I'm thinking about heading back to the interstate. Which is what I want to talk to you about. Bob said *we* could stay in the church basement if I take the Mike and Son job, and you take the one helping Merle in the church kitchen. I'm going over to the church from here to see what this space in the basement is all about."

"We'd live together?"

"Yes."

"A couple, like married."

Reggie mulled, then looked up. "Almost."

She dropped her head. It wasn't hard for Reggie to see the tear drop onto her lap. She wiped her eye.

"You okay with that?" Reggie asked.

"We've never even kissed."

Like it was scripted for a Hollywood romance movie, Reggie slipped off the cafeteria chair to one knee. He leaned in and kissed Sasha gently on the lips, then pulled away.

She gently pulled him back for another. "*Now* I'm okay with it."

Reggie grinned, leaned in for another, then got back onto his chair. "I'll go to the church and see what we're in for. Bob says even the dogs are welcome."

"You ready to take a job? Earn money? Pay taxes? Give up your freedom?"

"For now. We can't live under the ramp forever. This is, at the very least, a chance to pay our way while we decide what to do."

"We, huh."

"Yeah, we, us. You and me."

"And the dogs."

"Always."

"Reggie, I . . . like you a lot. Not sure I'm ready to say I love you, but it's crossed my mind."

"Mine, too, about you," he said. "Bob said something about patience. Guess that applies to love as well."

"You afraid?"

"Not sure. I mean, my mother and father should have loved me. If that's true, then love's not for me. But if what Bob and Trisha have is love, then I could get used to it."

She smiled. "Take me back to my room." She looked tired.

Reggie left the hospital. Bug had waited by the entry bench and joined him walking to the church. Bob was sweeping the front walkway in front of the church. He waved as Reggie approached.

"Come to see your new digs?"

"Maybe."

"How's Sasha?"

"Better. We walked and talked. Her armpits hurt from the crutches, ribs bother her, too. She's interested in Merle's offer. I guess I am, too. Let's go have a look at this basement."

Bob put an arm across Reggie's shoulders. Reggie started to resist, then relaxed and let it be. The wind swirled garden debris across the swept walkway.

Reggie got the whole tour. A small room further down a dark hall from the storage room where they'd been eating. A small bathroom, single bare light bulb with a pull chain hung from the middle of the ceiling. All of it filthy and badly stained. No window in the bath or small room.

"Sure, it needs some cleaning up, but that's what a strong back and good hands are for," Bob said.

Reggie knew he wasn't kidding. "Got any paint?" Reggie asked.

"Lots. All kinds of colors," Bob laughed. "Not enough of one to paint the whole room."

"I'll think on it. Sure feels confining, but it is out of the weather."

"Warm in winter," Bob said.

"Probably cool in summer," Reggie said.

"Yep," Bob replied. "What now?"

"Me and the dogs are going back to the ramp until Sasha is ready to leave the hospital. We'll wait there until then. I've got to think about all this."

"It's a lot for you, Reggie, I understand that. From what I've learned about you, this is a lot to commit to, but for you and your family, might be a good thing, for now."

"For now," Reggie sighed.

He left the church, walked to Bob's house, collected his family and traversed the streets back to West Lindsey, and his small camp under the interstate exit.

He and Bug scrambled to the Uncle Denny's dumpster for scraps. They returned with lots of goodies. Big, Buck, Black and Blue seemed excited to be back in their old space.

Bug was not so sure. He paced the the perimeter just out of the wind and rain.

In the middle of the night, Reggie was jolted upright from his sleep by the tornado siren.

Thirteen

The night exploded like a bomb. Lightning blew apart a tree towards the river. Lit the morning gloom.

Reggie lurched from the crumbling recess, stumbled forward to his hands and knees. He crawled against the wind to the edge of the ramp. Behind him, all five dogs, far more alert than Reggie, stayed close behind. Across West Lindsey, Uncle Denny's breakfast traffic was emptying as fast as they could exit the parking lot. Traffic on the interstate, all those commuters, was a mess. Small fender benders everywhere. Some folks abandoned their cars running for shelter.

A power line was down, transformers were blowing up everywhere. Sparks danced across the frontage road.

Reggie watched the Uncle Denny's night guy run from the back door to his car. Just as quick, he ran back inside. A car, out of control, side-swiped the back of the restaurant. Horns honked, people yelled. Thunder roared across the Oklahoma Plains.

Reggie came out from under the ramp, rain and wind buffeted him nearly off his feet. Valley Bank's digital clock said five-fifteen. He glared up at the dark sky, lightning bolted in three different places.

A swirling angry monster was about to drop from the sky.

Sasha!

Reggie turned, dropped, crawled back to the dogs.

"*Stay*! All of you stay right here. Me and Bug are going to get Sasha." He could barely hear himself scream.

He stood, bent in half, deciding which way to go. It was impossible to cross West Lindsey. He turned back with Bug. Together, they crawled under the interstate, raced across the frontage road to the forest of alders and his old campground. Nothing had changed.

The ground trembled like a sharp earthquake. Or something heavy had collapsed. Reggie's heart skipped a beat. He paused, clutched his stomach.

What now?

He stopped to listen. The wind roared through the alders. An eighteen-wheeler blared its horn, then there was a horrific crash.

He and Bug ran from the alders to the river's edge, stumbled along in the early dawn light until they came to where the interstate crossed over the river. At least twenty-five men, women and children huddled tight against the concrete bulkhead.

A small Mexican man yelled at him. "Get in here, Kid! Tornado could strike anywhere."

Tornado?

"Can't! I got someone I gotta help," Reggie yelled back, running close behind Bug, who seemed to know where they were going. He made it another four blocks, the hospital lights just ahead, when he looked back. Lightning lit the morning. The monster was chewing into the interstate behind him.

Shards of lightning cleaved the dark into several pieces. Some pieces exploded, sent sparks like fireworks high in the air. Some pieces twinkled down right on top of Reggie. He instinctively covered his head.

Bug barked, Reggie followed.

A transformer blew a half block ahead of Reggie and Bug. The pole it was on collapsed across the street. They took another route around the block. Power poles were falling one at a time down the block. A car was on fire.

The monster was devouring cars and homes, bikes, appliances, and people. Spitting them out like something was caught in its teeth.

Reggie veered further away from the hospital, away from the monster's claws. Rain pushed him back, Bug barked and kept barking to keep Reggie headed in the right direction.

The hospital was dead ahead.

Lightning lit the sky for several seconds, long enough for Reggie to stop and admire the dark looming twister bearing down on Norman.

"Shit, Bug, we're screwed," Reggie yelled.

He began checking car doors, locked. Another, locked. He set off the car alarm and ran. Around the next corner, an old van was parked in a driveway – unlocked.

Something wet and slimy hit Reggie in the neck. Bug barked. They jumped into the van, slid the side door closed. A chunk of wood blew apart the front windshield. Reggie and Bug hunkered down on the van's floor behind the middle bench seat.

Outside, a steady staccato of windswept garbage slammed into the van. Then, the van was airborne. Reggie cried out, held firm to the back of the seat and Bug. Noise outside was like the chugging drum of a locomotive engine roaring down the tracks.

The van bumped hard into something that cracked. It flipped and rolled, slammed into something hard enough to stop their movement. The van shimmied, scraped along until the it broke free and began spinning on its side. Hit another something, it cracked, exploded and sent sparks all over the van.

"Shit, Bug, we're dead."

Bug barked.

Reggie hit his head on the rear door of the van, the smell of blood filled the crumpled vehicle.

Bug barked.

They hit the ground, bounced and slammed into the front door of a small house. The old wooden porch buckled, collapsed down upon the van, Reggie and Bug.

Bug barked.

It grew quiet. Reggie didn't know much about tornadoes. Were they in the eye? No, that's a hurricane. Was it gone? He held his bleeding head. Found a beach towel, pressed it to the back of his head. Then his temple, bleeding like a son of a gun.

"You hurt, Bug?" Too dark to tell, but Bug barked, nuzzled Reggie.

"I'll take that as a no."

He tried the door, no good. None of the doors would open. From the windows, he figured whatever the van had hit, it had collapsed on the van. He was trapped inside.

"We gotta get to Sasha."

The van lay on its side. Reggie peeled back the floor liner, exposing the spare tire and lug wrench. He unhooked the wrench, broke out the rear window. Kicked at the splintered wood leaning against the van. Minutes later, he lifted Bug out of the broken window frame, slid through and stepped into the swirling rain.

A war zone.

He had no idea where he was in Norman. Nothing he saw before him was familiar. There wasn't much to see but smoke, fire, rain and crumpled piles of wood and sheet rock and glass where once homes sat.

And crying, screaming people.

"Where's my baby?"

Reggie cringed.

He and Bug stepped gingerly to a small, grass clearing. Part of a yard fence still stood. He looked a full three-sixty for the hospital. Found it, probably a quarter mile away. It stood out like a sore thumb, the only building still standing.

Fully engulfed in flames.

Sasha!

Amidst screams for help, sparks from downed lines and dizzy people crawling out of demolished structures, he and Bug started towards the burning hospital structure. He helped a man with his four children. They were looking for the mother.

"Where's my baby? Oh, God!"

Another man walked in a daze clutching a black and white cat. He was crying and calling out for Carol. Blocks later, Reggie pointed Carol in the right direction.

He stood outside the front of the burning hospital, sirens blared in the distance. There as lots of smoke.

He could hear voices, lots of them. People barking orders, running from the building with patients in wheelchairs, on gurneys. I.V. bottles chased along on poles gripped by a nurse or total stranger.

Reggie yelled her name.

"*Sasha!*"

He could hardly hear himself, felt a little ridiculous. He headed into the rubble. A man, bleeding from his forehead, came out the broken, front sliding door. "You can't go in there, Kid. There's fire everywhere."

Kid?

"My, my . . . my wife's in there," Reggie blurted. It sounded better than *friend*.

The man studied Reggie, who looked more like ten than the fifteen he would be, let alone, old enough to be married.

"Your wife, huh. Well, Kid, good luck. She ain't in there. If she is, say your prayers."

"What do you mean? Everybody dead?"

"No way. They moved all the in-patients to a bunker around back by the back-up generator. More likely she's there, but if she's in *that* hell hole, say your prayers."

"Thanks."

I think.

Reggie followed Bug, who ran like he knew where to go.

He did.

Some folks were already out of the bunker, milling about, staring at the burning hospital. Something exploded inside, a window blew out, folks moved farther away.

"Are there more inside?" Reggie asked a nurse.

"Yes, quite a few. Please help us get them out here," she said.

"Why not leave 'em in there outta the rain?"

"Generator's making weird noises. The hospital administrator has ordered us all into that field over . . ." She stopped there, looking past Reggie to the nearby field.

The field wasn't vacant. The nurse screamed.

A black, angry funnel was just forming and dropping to earth at the far end of the field, littered with swirling rubble.

The nurse screamed again and everyone turned to where she was looking, then all hell broke loose.

"*Bug!* Find Sasha."

The tornado siren went off, gurgled a moment and went silent. Lights that were on, blinked out. The emergency generator kicked, clanked and sparked. A man, gray hair, torn shirt, bleeding from an arm, came running out.

"Anyone who can, help us get these folks out."

Then he, along with the rest, watched the horror coming at them. It touch downed and began tossing whatever it consumed all over Norman.

"*Bug!*"

Like so many chickens with their heads cut off, screaming men, women and children ran for something to hide under. Most of those places were already beginning to shimmy and shake with the wind. Nurses, and others in scrubs, helped patients. Some raced back into the generator room. A thin column of white smoke drifted from the door. Others ran towards the black smoke billowing from the hospital.

Bug ran towards the hospital.

"Bug, it's on fire!" Reggie yelled, but he followed.

Bug raced up, over and around debris, broken glass and flying wreckage. He rounded a corner of the hospital onto a patio surrounded by a low, brick wall. Tables, chairs and a couple shade umbrellas bounced and skidded around the enclosure. Both doors to the cafeteria were gone, glass broken from one, the other just gone.

Bug, now barking with purpose, charged through the opening, Reggie right behind.

"*Help!*"

It wasn't Sasha, but a man in a wheelchair on its side. Reggie set him upright. "You see a girl down here? Short blond hair, my age."

He started to point, when Bug bolted towards a hallway leading deeper into the hospital.

"Shit!" Reggie ran, crunching glass as he went. They didn't go far. Bug clawed at a restroom door.

"Sasha?"

"In here."

Reggie opened the door. There she was, huddled on her wheelchair in the middle of the small restroom. She sobbed at the sight of Reggie and Bug.

"I-I wheeled down to the cafeteria for something. I just needed to get out of my room. Then something exploded and people ran. I couldn't make any headway with this leg cast. I brought my crutches in case I couldn't roll this thing. No one would help, so I ducked in here about the time the building started to shake. I smelled smoke."

"Tornado."

"So I figured."

"No, another one. Closing in on us right now."

Sasha clutched Reggie's hand like it was a lifeline, looked up at him for answers.

"Bug?" Reggie said, expecting the reliable dog to lead them to safety. Bug jumped behind the door and closed it.

To Sasha. "I think we're staying right here."

Tornado missed a direct hit, but it fanned the fire and ripped much of the landscape into a moonscape. When Reggie and Sasha emerged out the cafeteria doors, as far as they could see, Norman was gone.

"Where are the dogs?" Sasha asked.

"Safe under the West Lindsey exit ramp."

"Good, we should try to get there, too. It would be safest."

Reggie nodded he agreed then studied her. "I was so worried about you. When I saw all the smoke coming from the building, well, I was worried."

"All I could think about was you," Sasha said. They kissed, quick, but meaningful.

Bug barked.

"I can't carry you very far," Reggie said. "Let's take the wheelchair. I'll carry you when we can't use it anymore."

"If we can find some crutches, I can walk some, too. I'm much better, weak, but better. Where are we going?"

"Bob's house isn't far. We should check on them. 'Sides, it's on the way to the interstate ramp."

Fourteen

Bug started barking when they were two blocks down the street from Bob's. Most of the houses on his block were gone, but for a few chimneys, porches, foundations. Bob's picket fence was gone except the gate, swinging in the wind. Sky was getting brighter, no more monsters, but the rain persisted.

"You think they survived?" Sasha asked, tears running down her face.

"Yep. If they tossed out all the toys and stuff."

"What's *that* mean?"

"Bug, find Bob."

Still a block away from Bob's, Bug barked. There was a return bark. Ahead, a black and white border collie sat expectantly, his tail wagging.

"It's Blue," Reggie yelled. "*Damn!* She shouldn't be here."

Reggie ran, pushing the wheelchair ahead of him. The going was difficult. Bug and Blue were happy to see each other. Blue whined for Reggie and Sasha to follow. She pawed the earth, clawed at a two-by-four on top of a wood pile where Bob's living room once was. Reggie jumped in, tossing aside whatever he touched.

"Bob? Trisha?"

Blue scrambled, but not at the shelter Bob had shown Reggie. This was more towards the back of the house.

"*Bob!* Where are you?"

Blue howled like she was in pain. Reggie scrambled over wood and sheet rock, Bob's refrigerator.

"In here."

Blue frantically dug.

"In here," Bob sounded either hurt or in trouble. Or both.

Both.

Once Reggie had pulled back the wall and squeezed himself between large pieces of roof and broken trusses, he found Trisha and the two boys safely huddled in the bath tub. Bob was crammed in between the toilet and the tub.

There was a lot of Bob really crammed into a small space.

The top of his head was bleeding. Trisha was in tears, the boys too stunned to cry, pale. The kitchen stove rested on Bob's legs wedged tight under the pile.

Reggie helped Trisha from the tub. She quickly dropped to the floor to hug Bob, kissed his head and neck. Said lots of nice things about how he saved them.

How she loved him.

Weak and crippled as she was, on one crutch Sasha struggled to get the boys out of the tub and into the open grass nearby. There was no wall between the bathroom and the lawn.

Reggie sat on the floor with Bob and Trisha.

"You can tell us all about it later. I need to get that stove off your legs. Trisha, I'll need your help. I'll leverage something to lift it, you pull Bob out."

They got it done. Nothing broken, but both legs were badly bruised.

"I think they're both bent," Bob said to lighten the moment.

"Funny, Big Man," Trisha said. "You were *damn* lucky, pardon my French."

"Yes, I was. We all were. How'd you find us so quick?" He asked Reggie.

"Blue. She brought us right to where you were. I figured you to be in the shelter, but Blue knew otherwise," Reggie said, looking for the black and white border collie. "Anyone see her?"

Bug barked.

"Well, she'll be around. Bug's here."

Bug barked again, grabbed Reggie's hand and tugged.

"Bug wants to take me somewhere else. Bob, you guys okay?"

"We are now."

"Unless there's another one," Trisha interrupted.

They all nodded, Reggie and Sasha, feeling stronger by the minute, dropped in behind Bug. Reggie kept a constant lookout for Blue.

Reggie pushed the wheelchair as fast as he could. They met Nancy in her wheelchair out front of Mike and Son Masonry. She'd been crying. Her house and the business shop were intact. The tornado had curled around the neighborhood. The monster couldn't eat a stone house anyway.

Nancy cried out as they approached. "It's Merle. He went to the new construction site to take some measurements before ordering tile. I can't reach him on his cell phone." She burst into tears.

"Where is it?"

Bug barked, tugged.

"Never mind, we'll follow Bug. If he's there, we'll find him."

For a long distance, the streets and sidewalks were clear. No tornado damage and the going was easy, especially for Sasha in the wheelchair. But ahead, it wasn't hard to tell Mother Nature had dropped a weather bomb on another part of Norman.

Just at the fringe of more disaster, Buck sat as if waiting for them. Straight up, tail wagging.

"Buck, Buddy."

More joy.

The little terrier started weaving through the carnage towards the obvious new construction site. A pile of two-by-fours, mangled trusses and framing. Merle's truck was upside down in a nearby ravine.

Buck sniffed a moment at the smashed driver's side window, barked, and raced around to the other side. He skidded down the embankment to a thin stream of water, then up the other side.

Jumped a tree trunk and disappeared into piles of broken trees and brush.

Buck barked.

Bug replied.

Reggie yelled. "Merle?"

"Here."

Reggie raced to Merle's voice, Sasha couldn't follow.

Merle was flat on his back. A spear-like tree limb was embedded in his shoulder. Another larger branch lay across his right leg. He couldn't move.

"*Reggie!* Oh, thank you, Jesus. Boy, am I glad to see you. How in the hell did you find me out here?"

"Your mother sent us to this site, but Buck brought us right to you. You see him?"

"Buck? That the little terrier?"

"Yes," said Sasha, hobbling on her crutches towards them. She scanned the field for the little dog.

"Buck! Here, Boy."

"Probably looking for more folks needin' help," Merle said. "How's Mother?"

"She's fine. The twister missed your house and shop. Your neighbors were missed, too," Sasha said. "But your truck's ruined."

"Travois," Reggie said. "We'll build us a travois and haul him back to his house."

"I can call an ambulance to get me to the hospital from there," Merle said.

Reggie chuckled, glanced over at Sasha, then back to Merle. "Hospital's gone, well, it's standing, but on fire. We'll get you back to your house. Maybe your mother and Sasha can temporarily patch you up."

"Merle?" Sasha shook him. "Reggie, he's gone into shock. Seen it before and he's in shock."

"Crap. We gotta move."

It took Reggie ten minutes to scramble together a makeshift travois. They had Merle on his couch twenty minutes later.

Reggie carefully removed the broken piece of tree branch stuck in Merle's shoulder, then the two women went to work to stop the bleeding. From time-to-time, Nancy called 9-1-1 on her cell phone.

Reggie kissed Sasha, now too tired and weak to go on, but he knew he had to. "Gotta check on the dogs. Then we'll all come back here."

Fifteen

It took Reggie nearly an hour for him and Bug to reach sight of the interstate, West Lindsey was impassable. He took another route out to the river hoping to reach the exit ramp from the back way. Some parts of the open fields were clear, others were piled high with crushed cars, furniture, appliances, pieces of homes and everything imaginable. Reggie reached the river. It had overflowed its banks, filled the low ravines and some fields.

Reggie heard barking nearby.

Bug barked, too.

A car rested upside down, half in and out of the rising water. And a voice weakly called for help from inside the very familiar old blue Oldsmobile.

By the driver's side door, Black sat, barking for all she was worth. Like all labs, her tail was going like a metronome. She sat with a slight wiggle that labs do, her lips curled up to smile.

The smile was genuine, Black was special.

Reggie went to hug her, but she bolted off around the half buried car before he could reach her.

Sure like to hug them for all they're doing, Reggie thought.

Bug barked.

"*Help!*"

Reggie dropped to his knees, bent down to look inside the Olds. He swung around and sat cross-legged staring into Buster O'Connell's bloody face. His sparse mustache no worse for wear.

"*Help!*" Buster cried. "You have to help me!"

"Don't *have* to," Reggie said. He folded his arms across his chest, smirked at the irony.

O'Connell swung his head away from Reggie.

"What's the matter? You think I'm a ghost come back to haunt you? This big-ass pile of shit you call a car didn't *kill* either of us. I should leave you here just another tornado casualty."

"You can't do that!"

"Sure I can. Should set it on fire. Who'd know?"

Reggie was now red with anger.

"You would."

Reggie nodded, he knew Buster was right.

But he's such an asshole.

His heart softened some, Bug nudged at him, then barked. How could he just leave a man to die? Even this one. The river kept rising. Bug sat poised, nearby and barked. Reggie's four-legged conscience.

Mustache mumbled up at Reggie. "I got a knife in my pocket. Can't get it, but you could. You could cut this seat belt and haul me out."

Reggie didn't say anything, just pulled the knife from Buster's back pocket and cut the strap and pulled. Buster screamed like Reggie had buried the knife in his eyeball, both his arms were broken. His back, too. He had bloody gashes on his head and face.

"I'm really screwed up," Buster said, his voice faded.

"Can't carry you. I'll have to drag you, and it'll hurt like hell. I'll move you to higher ground and get help out to you as soon as they can."

"I could die out here," Buster whined.

"You could, but you won't. You're too damn mean for that. Hang on, I'll do what I said."

"Sasha, she okay?"

"What do you care?"

"Sorry for what I did. I was pretty torqued at you two for what happened to my brother. Is she alright?"

"Yes."

Mustache nodded he was glad.

Reggie tugged Buster to a high spot in the field. Pulled a tarp from the Olds' trunk and covered him.

"Tell you what, Mustache . . ."

"Mustache?"

"Yeah, Sasha never got your name, so we called you Mustache. Your brother, Gaunt. He was kinda skinny and pale."

"His name was Mitch."

"Mitch, okay, then. As I was saying, I'll get help out here quick as I can if you promise to leave me and Sasha alone."

He nodded he would, then blinked sleepy like.

Bug barked. He was alone, Black faded away into the tall grass.

Reggie continued along the river's edge, crossed back where he thought he could wade across the swift current. He carried Bug. They made it, but their sideways direction with the current took them far downstream from the campsite. He dropped Bug on the slope. Above them, looking down, his big ears dropping forward, sat a huge mound of gray fur.

"*Big!*"

The huge dog trotted halfway down, his wiggle so familiar to Reggie.

"C'mon. Let's get the others and head for Merle's."

Big barked. Bug, once again, mouthed Reggie's hand. They led him away along the riverbank until they reached where the interstate passed close to the frontage road. There was no traffic, mostly crashed cars, trees, and more parts of Norman strewn all over.

Big barked.

Bug pushed at Reggie. Big led the way.

Reggie followed through the twisted up cyclone fence along the interstate. Stayed right behind Big through the tangled mess spread across the six lanes. Paramedics, firemen everywhere helping folks.

"Hey, who do I talk to about a guy in the field north of the river behind Safeway?"

"Is he hurt?" The fireman asked.

"Lots of cuts and two broken arms. He said something about his back. I couldn't carry him, but he's near an old blue Oldsmobile that's half in the river."

"Friend of yours?"

"Not really," Reggie said straight faced.

"I'll get someone out there as soon as I can. Good job, Kid."

Kid?

"Thanks," Reggie said.

Big barked and grabbed Reggie's hand.

They hurried across the rest of the interstate, then down the embankment to the frontage road on the other side. Big began to run, Bug right behind. Reggie, exhausted, did what he could to keep up. The two dogs stopped at a big green dumpster in a mountain of twisted cars and light poles.

Bug barked, Big, too.

"Hello? Anyone in there?"

No reply.

"Hello?"

Nothing.

"You two missed this one. Nobody in there."

Bug grabbed his hand again and bit hard.

"Ouch! Shit, Bug, no biting."

Big barked.

"Okay, what? Where?"

Big circled the pile, Bug, too.

Big climbed up, clawed at the dumpster. Reggie shook his head, but climbed up. He peered inside. It was empty of any garbage or food scraps. Empty except for the Uncle Denny's guy, battered, bleeding and unconscious.

"*Hey!*" Yelled Reggie. The man didn't move.

"Stay with him, you two. I'll get a paramedic." Reggie ran back to the interstate. A paramedic followed him back. Jumped inside the dumpster.

"He's alive, Kid. You just may have saved this one's life."

Kid?

"Good," Reggie said.

Reggie turned to the dogs, both were gone. He ran to West Lindsey, crossed. Started to run towards the exit ramp, then stumbled to a stop.

His heart stopped.

The wind ceased.

The spinning world screeched to a halt.

Ahead, more twisted cars and trucks, a bus, bales of barb wire, and all manner of garbage and vegetation lay tangled and heaped over and around the interstate.

And a collapsed exit ramp onto West Lindsey.

Bug sat facing him in front of the huge slab of freeway resting flat on the ground. It should have been elevated high in the air.

It should have been!

Reggie sank.

Stay right here, he had told them.

They trusted him. Did what he asked.

Be right back, he had promised.

But they had followed, one at a time. Helped find Bob and his family. Merle. That asshole, Mustache.

Saved the nice Uncle Denny's guy who'd been feeding them all these months.

Where were the dogs now?

Bug barked and ran to Reggie's side. Together they walked towards the heap of concrete and asphalt. Reggie stood in the grass before it. His secret recess now clearly exposed for all to see.

"You okay, Kid?" A fireman asked.

Startled, Reggie jumped. "Y-yes. *No!* Um, when did this collapse?" He fought back the tears, shied back at what the answer might be.

"Eyewitnesses said the first tornado made landfall right here. Hit this overpass like a hundred tons of bricks. It just crumbled to the ground."

"How long ago?"

"Well, first tornado was maybe three hours ago. Five fifteen, five thirty maybe. You sure you're okay?"

"No."

Reggie looked down at Bug.

Bug barked.

Sixteen

Stunned at the possibility his four-legged family lay under tons of asphalt and concrete, Reggie and Bug sat by the slab for a long time. Around them, ambulances, firemen and policemen from surrounding towns and cities, converged on the disaster scene. News media swarmed like hungry bees.

Sasha tapped his shoulder and sat next to him. Bob and his family crept up behind. Sasha knew they were gone, they all did. Not much to be said.

Bob inched up, knelt next to Reggie, put an arm over the boy's shoulders. Before he could speak, a paramedic ran up from behind.

"Hey, Kid!"

Reggie, everyone, turned.

"That guy in the dumpster? He'll be okay. Says to thank you and that big gray dog. You two probably saved his life."

Reggie nodded that was good, smiled, but it was a grim smile. Bob squeezed his shoulder.

No one spoke.

Finally, Bob dropped on his butt, sat facing Reggie and Sasha. Bug cuddled in, too.

"We talked to Merle and Nancy on their way to Oklahoma City in an ambulance. The paramedic said Merle lost so much blood, he wouldn't have lasted much longer. You and Buck saved him."

Reggie dropped his head into his hands. Sobbing in big heaves. "Not fair," he blubbered.

"No, it's not," Bob said, now crying, too. "Not even close to fair. Something like this never is."

An ambulance bounced over the curb behind them. Splashed across the mud and grass, stopped. Two paramedics got out.

"One of you called Sasha?"

"I am," Sasha said.

She stayed on the ground holding tight to Reggie's hand.

"We got a guy in here in the ambulance who insists on seeing you and your boyfriend. He saw you from the ambulance while we waited to get through the traffic. He's hurt real bad, so keep it quick."

Sasha and Reggie shrugged at one another and followed to the ambulance. The paramedic swung open the rear door.

Mustache, thought Sasha.

Buster, thought Reggie.

With the help of the other paramedic, Buster lifted his head. Peered down his battered body, over his feet out the back of the ambulance. "I ain't much good at this, but thanks. You and that nice black lab probably saved my life. You didn't have to. I guess I owe you."

Reggie leaned in. "You don't owe me anything, but the lab? Yes, *she* saved your life."

"Thank her for me."

"I . . . I will. And remember our deal."

"I will."

The paramedic elbowed in. "That's enough, guys. We gotta get him to the city pronto." He slammed the doors and they were gone.

"So, Black found this guy?" Sasha asked.

"Yeah, just like the others found everybody else."

"But . . ." Sasha paused, squinted at the slab of fallen ramp, then back at Reggie, confused.

If they were under the slab, then . . . ? She wondered.

Reggie looked up into her amazing face, tears jumped from his eyes. "Sasha, this ramp dropped four hours ago. Right after me and Bug left the dogs to go find you. I told them to stay put."

Reggie paused, choked at the sound of his own voice, at images of Blue, Black, Big and Buck.

"*I* told them to stay! *I'm* the one who did this to them."

Sasha hugged him.

"And they stayed, Reggie. It's not your fault. They loved you so much," she whispered and turned to the slab again. "But if they stayed, then . . ."

"Kids?"

Sasha and Reggie turned to Pastor Bob, his clothes were torn, bloody and covered in dirt and grass stains. Somehow, his white preacher's collar was still pristine white as the day it was new.

Bug barked.

Bob had been listening. "You three must be looking for answers?" Bob sniffled, Trisha at his side.

Reggie nodded he was.

Bug barked.

"I guess we are," Sasha said. "We're missing something here."

Then it hit Pastor Bob, like a ton of Bibles. He nodded with a sliver grin like he knew the answer, then crumpled in a heap and started to cry uncontrollably.

Trisha moved up to him, kissed Bob's tear-stained cheek. To Reggie and Sasha. "Bob knows what happened, he *really* does. It's all about . . . angels.

"Angels?" Reggie said.

"He'll explain another day," Trisha said. "You'll have to trust him."

"I do," Reggie said.

Bug barked.

It was a joyous bark.

End

Made in the USA
Columbia, SC
22 April 2017